KT-386-313

PUFFIN BOOKS

THE CATASTROPHIC FRIENDSHIP FAILS OF LOTTIE BROOKS

KATIE KIRBY

PUFFIN

PUFFIN BOOKS

UK | USA | Canada | Ireland | Australia
India | New Zealand | South Africa

Puffin Books is part of the Penguin Random House group of companies
whose addresses can be found at global.penguinrandomhouse.com.

www.penguin.co.uk   www.puffin.co.uk   www.ladybird.co.uk

First published 2022
005

Text and illustrations copyright © Katie Kirby, 2022

The moral right of the author/illustrator has been asserted

The brands mentioned in this book are trademarks belonging to third parties

Text design by Kim Musselle
Printed and bound in Great Britain by Clays Ltd, Elcograf S.p.A.

The authorized representative in the EEA is Penguin Random House Ireland,
Morrison Chambers, 32 Nassau Street, Dublin D02 YH68

A CIP catalogue record for this book is available from the British Library

ISBN: 978-0-241-46090-0

All correspondence to:
Puffin Books
Penguin Random House Children's
One Embassy Gardens, 8 Viaduct Gardens, London SW11 7BW

MIX
Paper from
responsible sources
FSC® C018179
www.fsc.org

Penguin Random House is committed to a
sustainable future for our business, our readers
and our planet. This book is made from Forest
Stewardship Council® certified paper.

To Zoë Telford-Reed, for
sending me my first-ever
piece of fan mail and
making my day!

FRIDAY 21 JANUARY

I'm back! Sorry it's been **SO** long but I have finally
purchased a new diary and I am looking forward to
filling you in on all my exciting adventures . . . or I guess
embarrassing adventures if we are being entirely honest,
which is our thing, right?

oh so
Shiny and
New

PRIVATE
PROPERTY
of LOTTIE
BROOKS
KEEP OUT OR
fACE SEVERE
CONSEQUENCES

(I've not figured out what the consequences will be yet but
trust me - and I'm speaking to you here, Toby - you won't want
to find out!)

Anyway, did you miss me?

No?!

Well, that's a bit rude!

Only kidding.

I guess it's only been about a week, but it feels like longer **IYSWIM** because **A LOT** has happened since we last 'met'. How about a handy list to fill you all in, eh?

OK, here we go. Stuff that has happened in the last week includes:

> * Mum's still in hospital, but she's finally
>   coming home tomorrow. We've been to visit
>   my new baby sister, Davina – I mean **BELLA**
>   (must get that right!) – a couple of times and
>   she is très cute! I mean, she doesn't do much
>   yet, but I guess we need to give her time as
>   she's still only ten days old.

* It's been **SO** wonderful having Molly back from Australia – we've seen each other almost every day and it's just like old times!

* Amber and Poppy have been mostly staying out of my way. Phew.

* I'm kinda still a *little* bit keen on Daniel. Like a real *tiny* bit. Almost *nothing* really.

* I absolutely do not spend loads of time sitting at my desk daydreaming about him and drooling all over my diary.

I <u>NEVER</u>
do this

* Oh, who am I even kidding? I **REALLY** like him. But shhhh, don't tell anyone, OK.

* Argh, and now I have **ACTUALLY** drooled on the page! Maybe if I give the drool a face it'll look less disgusting?!

Hi I'm a blob of drool called Nigel!

urgh soz I'm so gross!

* Why do I ramble so much?! One minute I'm giving you an update on my life and the next I'm banging on about Nigel the Blob of Drool. What were we even talking about again?

* Oh, yeh . . . Dreamy Daniel! (He's soooo nice.)

* I might need you to occasionally shout **'GET A GRIP, LOTTIE!'** if I start going on about him too much – promise? I'll pretend you said 'yes' – thank you.

* Hmmm. What else? The hamsters are still as **CUTE AS EVER**. I bet you missed them more than me, huh? They are extra delighted right now because I got them some new hammocks for their cage . . .

PS Hamsters absolutely deserve to live their best lives because their life expectancy is only two to three years on average, which seems incredibly unfair. But shhhhhh, don't tell Fuzzball the 3rd and Professor Squeakington that as I don't want them to get upset.

PPS I've drawn them with cocktails because I thought it was funny but, just to be clear, hamsters **DO NOT** drink alcohol. If you start putting gin and tonic in their water bottle, then I have a feeling that they may live A LOT less than two to three years. Also, your parents might be very cross with you for stealing their precious gin. You have been warned!

SATURDAY 22 JANUARY

9.45 a.m.

Today's the day Mum comes home! I cannot wait. I mean, at first it was kind of fun having Dad being the only parent because he was much more relaxed about certain things like putting dirty clothes in the laundry bin, making beds, homework and (mostly) screen time. He's just super gullible – he'd say things like, 'How long have you been on your iPad, Lottie?' and I'd go, 'Oh, only about five minutes, Dad,' and he'd go, 'Oh, that's fine – carry on then.'

Usually I'd been on for about two hours! Sucker.

The downside was his cooking. Not that he didn't try. I wish he hadn't tried and had just served us nuggets and pizza – that would have been fine. The problem was that he was so keen to show Mum what an 'amazing husband and dad' he was that he kept trying to cook things **WAY** beyond his means and then getting it spectacularly wrong.

I mean, last weekend he tried to do a Sunday lunch without purchasing any of the vital ingredients. Like a chicken or a joint of beef. So, we had 'roast fish', which was basically incinerated salmon covered in gravy. It wasn't even a fillet – it was one of those whole ones with a face and everything!

Me and Toby were traumatized, I tell you!

In fact, I'm still having nightmares about it now . . . often really strange ones where the salmon's got funny little arms and is playing a tiny guitar. It's super weird.

Hmmm . . . maybe I was being a little unkind, but I just don't want to sing songs with a dead aquatic animal when I'm trying to get my beauty sleep, OK? The fact that Mr Fishy could play a blimmin' good version of Harry Styles' 'Watermelon Sugar' is beside the point!

Wahoo, she's back! There are now five people living in this house, which seems insane. Or seven if you count hamsters as people, which I actually do.

I mean, they are more competent at most things than Toby so that's got to count for something, right?

Anyway, I've been cuddling Bella all afternoon. She smells amazing, a bit like a strawberry milkshake, *mmmmm*.

Mum looks a bit different though, like really tired.

I said, 'Wow, Mum, you look tired!'

She said, 'Thanks, Lottie.'

'Yeh . . . you've got really big bags under your eyes.'

'Mmm . . . Thanks, Lottie.'

'And dark circles too . . . Also your skin looks kind of grey.'

'Thanks very much, Lottie.'

'You look quite a lot older actually . . .'

'YES, OK, YOU'VE MADE YOUR POINT NOW. THANK YOU, LOTTIE!'

I said, 'Geez, Mum. There's no need to shout. I was only making an observation!'

I guess maybe having a baby ages you or something . . .

Mum before Bella

Mum now :-/

I don't know why though . . . So far it all looks easy to me as all they seem to do is sleep.

THOUGHT OF THE DAY:
Remember to buy Mum some
rejuvenating anti-ageing face cream
for her birthday. She'll love that.

SUNDAY 23 JANUARY

Just woke up to a truly disturbing noise. Sounded a bit like a squirrel being beaten up by a fox. That might be a bit of a weird analogy though, because, come to think of it, I'm not sure I've ever heard a squirrel make a noise. Must look that up later.

I went to investigate and turns out it was Bella! I was flabbergasted (love that word). I mean, how can one teeny-tiny baby make that much sound?!

'What is it, Mum? What's wrong with her?!' I said.

'She's hungry, love. She just needs some milk.'

'Can she not wait until breakfast like a normal person?'

Mum laughed. 'Unfortunately not, Lottie. Babies have

very small tummies, so they need to eat very frequently to begin with.'

All seems pretty uncivilized to me.

4.47 a.m.

Couldn't sleep because I kept thinking about the squirrel question. Crept downstairs to look it up on my phone – yes, my mum is one of those annoying people who bans phones in the bedroom (except for hers, of course, which she is allowed to look at 24/7 – unfair).

If you are interested, I found out that squirrels do actually have a wide range of vocal features, including squeaks, grunts and barks. Fascinating!

I'm still finding it hard to sleep though, as I don't like to think of squirrels barking – it seems rather uncouth.

I was rudely woken up by Dad shaking me. 'Lottie, wake up! It's OK. I'm here.'

'What's going on?!' I was really confused.

'I thought you were having a nightmare!'

'No . . . I was just dreaming that I was a . . . squirrel.'

It was a rather nice dream TBF. Certainly nicer than being threatened by Mr Fishy and his tiny guitar anyway.

'Oh, right . . . well, I guess that's OK then. It just sounded a bit like you were barking.'

'Oh, ha ha . . . no. You must have been mistaken.'

God, I'm weird.

4.12 p.m.

Man alive, babies can make quite a lot of noise.

Bella seems to have stopped sleeping all the time and replaced it with crying all the time.

She has now been screaming for two solid hours. Nothing anyone does seems to help.

I asked Mum what was wrong with her this time and she said, 'I think she needs a burp.'

Imagine crying for hours because you need a burp. I mean, just get it outta ya, girl – we're all family here!

5.47 p.m.

Other things that Bella cries about . . .

* Being hungry

* Getting changed

* Having a bath

* Being put in her basket

* Going to sleep

* Waking up

* Doing a poo

* Doing a fart

* Loads of other stuff that no one has any clue about

I mean, talk about being melodramatic!

Just had a shower, was all fresh, clean and smelling like a daisy field, when Mum said, 'Can you hold Bella for a minute, Lottie? I just need a wee.'

I said, 'Sure, no probs,' like the helpful daughter I am.

Next thing I knew . . .

BLURGH.

ABSOLUTELY COVERED IN BABY VOM.

Toby's comments absolutely, categorically, didn't help.

So I had to have another shower as I didn't want to turn up to school tomorrow smelling like a mouldy bowl of cereal that's been left under the bed for two months (which I've obviously never done).

FYI I've definitely changed my opinion now – babies are absolutely minging!

MONDAY 24 JANUARY

I don't think I'd ever woken up feeling glad it was a
Monday morning, but today I was pretty glad to get out
of this noisy madhouse because, in comparison to being
at home, school feels like going on a spa break.

Also it was a really great day because I got some super-
exciting news . . .

I was sitting in registration chatting to Jess about our
favourite flavours of Pot Noodle – mine is Chicken and
Mushroom (which is weird as I hate mushrooms IRL
but I pick them out) followed by Beef and Tomato. Hers
are Chinese Chow Mein and Bombay Bad Boy. I was
impressed – I've always thought Bombay Bad Boy would
be way too spicy, but maybe I'll give it a try.

Anyway, I'm digressing. What was I talking about
again??

OH YES! The mega-exciting news – our Pot Noodle discussion was interrupted when my phone buzzed. It was a text from Molly.

MOLLY: OMG GUESS WHAT! I GOT A PLACE AT KINGSWOOD!!!!!

ME: OMG!!!!!! NO WAY!!!!!!!

MOLLY: YES WAY!!!!!! AND GUESS WHAT???????

ME: WHAT?!???!?

MOLLY: I'M GONNA BE IN YOUR FORM ROOM!!!!

ME: OMG NO WAYYYYYYYYYYYYYYYYYYYYYYYYYY!!!!!

I mean, maybe we overdid the caps a bit but, crikey, I was a bit excited!

'What is it? What is it? Tell me!!' begged Jess, trying to get a look over my shoulder.

'It's Molly. She's starting here next week!'

'Oh, wow! That's amazing! I can't wait to meet her.'

I grinned because having my two very best friends in the same class is going to be the **BEST THING EVER**.

'What are you two squealing about?' said Amber, leaning over to find out what all the commotion was about.

Part of me just wanted to tell her to mind her own business, but I'm determined to be a bigger person than that this year.

Lottie 2.0
The extra-mature version!

(NB I don't mean extra mature as in the type of cheddar . . .
I don't smell of cheese . . . I hope!)

'I just got a text from my best friend Molly. She's going to
be joining Seven Green next week,' I explained.

'Your **BEST** friend?' she said. 'I thought Jess was your
BEST friend.'

'Well, she is . . . They both are. You can have two best
friends, you know . . .'

'Really?' she said, smirking. 'You know what they say . . . Three's a crowd!'

'I don't care what they say. It's going to be brilliant.'

Amber gave me her best bored look. 'Yeh well, whatever. She's probably a total geek like you guys anyway.'

'Ignore her,' whispered Jess. 'She's just trying to get a reaction.'

I sighed. 'I know.'

'So . . .' said Jess. 'When am I finally going to get to meet the famous Molly?'

I frowned. I couldn't believe I'd not introduced them yet, but so much had been going on in the last week that there had literally been no time! What with catching up with Molly and visiting Mum in hospital, I'd been busy every day after school.

'How about Thursday?' I suggested. 'Come round to mine and you can meet her AND Bella!'

'I can't wait!'

When I got home, I told Mum I'd invited Molly and Jess over. She looked a bit put out to be honest.

'I've just got out of hospital, love. Can't it wait a while?'

'**NO!** It's super urgent, Mum. Molly and Jess haven't met yet and they are the two most important people in my **ENTIRE LIFE!**'

'Well, thanks very much!'

'Apart from my family of course.'

'Glad to hear it. OK, love, I'm sure we'll manage. What's another two mouths to feed, hey?'

'**YAY!** You are the BEST mum I've EVER had.'

'How many mums have you had?!'

'Oh, yeh. Good point.'

TUESDAY 25 JANUARY

I've come to the conclusion that I just can't talk to boys, and by boys I really mean Daniel. When I try, it's like my mouth is full of jam and none of the words come out right. Take today, for example . . .

Actually, before I tell you about that, here's a brief recap on the me-and-Daniel situ (just in case you didn't read my first diary) . . .

* We first met in science class and before long he started saying hi and smiling at me when I saw him. Eek!

* He asked me to dance at the autumn disco but, because I was so gassy after drinking too many fizzy drinks, I couldn't reply in case I burped in his face.

* I started worrying that maybe I'd blown it . . .

* But then he followed me on Instagram – OMG!

* He said I looked cute in my 'cute lil' cupcake' swimming costume even though I looked like a deranged ballerina.

* I started thinking maybe he liked me!

* Then he got a bit cold with me after I fell out with Jess. ☹

* After me and Jess patched things up he sent me a text saying 'Happy Christmas!'

* He started smiling at me again – YAY! ☺

* After we came back from the school holidays I suddenly noticed that he was super-extra hot and the rest, as they say, is history.

Cut back to present day

Where was I again? Oh, yeh. Talking to boys, urgh.

So, we had science first thing this morning. I always feel a bit nervous as I know I'm going to be seeing Daniel – he sits just behind me.

As I walked in, this is how the convo went. Please don't laugh . . .

I mean . . . LANIEL?!?

Sigh.

Worse still, Poppy and Amber heard too and burst into a fit of giggles. They were whispering about me throughout the whole lesson.

'Did you hear what she said?' sniggered Poppy.

'I know . . . *Laniel?* So embarrassing!' said Amber.

I didn't want them to have the satisfaction of knowing they had got to me, so I pretended to be utterly enthralled listening to Mrs Murphy talk about the chemical composition of a banana. Inside, however, all I wanted to do was crawl into a hole and hibernate for like **SEVENTY-EIGHT SQUILLION** years.

WEDNESDAY 26 JANUARY

Tomorrow is the big day when I introduce Molly and
Jess to each other, and I can't stop thinking about it. I
should be excited about my two BFFs finally meeting, but
instead I feel kind of nervous. I can't quite work it out –
what do I have to feel nervous about?

'What do they mean when they say *three's a crowd?*' I
asked Dad while shovelling Coco Pops into my mouth at
breakfast.

'Have you not heard the saying, love? It goes: *two's
company, three's a crowd.* It's just that quite often in a
group of three, you may get someone feeling a bit left
out because two of the people get on better together,
that's all.'

'Oh,' I said.

'Why do you ask?'

'Nothing . . . just something someone mentioned at school.'

I pushed my bowl away. I was getting an uneasy feeling in my tummy. What a waste of good Coco Pops though, and they weren't even supermarket own brand!

THURSDAY 27 JANUARY

7.01 a.m.

Didn't sleep well last night. I finally figured out why I'm feeling so nervous. It's because I love both Molly and Jess to death, but what if they don't like each other?

Damn Amber for putting these stupid thoughts in my head.

I looked at myself in the mirror to give myself a bit of a talking-to: 'Look – listen, Lottie, it's going to be fine! We are all grown-ups now (sort of).'

I turned to the hammies for backup – but they weren't very reassuring . . .

It's going to be OK right, guys?!

Na, you're deluding yourself!

Got any more strawberries, love?!

6.25 p.m.

Well, that went OK. I think.

I mean it was a bit awkward in parts, but nothing is ever perfect, right?

When me and Jess got home from school, Mum was in a right tizz.

'Lottie, I've not had time to even think about dinner today so I'm just going to have to order you a pizza, I'm afraid.'

'Nothing to be worried about, Mum. We are **MORE** than happy to pass on a home-cooked meal,' I said, winking at Jess.

'Thank you, Lotts. Now listen – will you girls look after Bella for fifteen minutes while I give the place a quick hoover?'

I still don't get why adults are so obsessed with hoovering. I **NEVER** notice crumbs on the floor, but they seem to make my mum super stressed.

'Sure thing, Mrs Brooks,' said Jess. 'Can I hold her?'

'OF COURSE!' said Mum, perhaps a bit too keenly. 'And call me Laura.'

'Make sure you support her head,' I instructed as Mum passed Bella to Jess.

'Oooooooh my gosh, she's so tiny and adorable,' cooed Jess.

'Just wait till you smell her head!' I said, feeling like a very proud big sister.

She sniffed her hair. **'STRAWBERRY MILKSHAKE!'**

'I know, right,' I said, laughing.

Just then the doorbell rang.

'That must be Molly,' I said, feeling a familiar lurch in my tummy.

'*Please let this work out OK*,' I said to myself, and I pulled the door open.

'HEY, BESTIE!' Molly said, giving me a hug.

'Hey yourself.' I smiled. 'Jess is already here.'

'Great.'

We walked through to the lounge where Jess was still sitting cuddling Bella.

'Sooooo . . . Molly, this is Jess, and, Jess, this is Molly,' I said, butterflies flitting around in my tummy.

'Hi, Jess,' said Molly, cool as anything. 'It's so good to finally meet you.'

'It's lovely to meet you too, Molly! I've just met Bella for the first time as well. Isn't she gorgeous?'

'Very! And have you smelt her head?'

'Yep . . . strawberry milkshake, right?'

They both started laughing and I grinned. The knot in my stomach was easing – I knew everything was going to be OK.

I never really had anything to worry about. It was just stupid Amber putting stupid thoughts in my head.

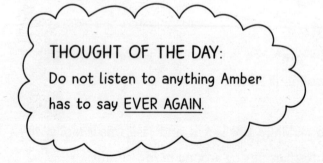

THOUGHT OF THE DAY:
Do not listen to anything Amber
has to say <u>EVER AGAIN</u>.

SATURDAY 29 JANUARY

Went to New Look with Jess and Molly. None of us had any money so we just went to try on stuff. We did that thing where we all pick each other outfits – the more ridiculous, the better.

It was pretty annoying though, because no matter what we chose for Molly she just looked incredible, whereas more often than not me and Jess looked kind of goofy. She even managed to make a plain black T-shirt dress look amazing.

Jess goes, 'Molly, that makes you almost look like a proper adult!'

'It's because you have actual boobs,' I agreed, suddenly noticing how much older she looked since she came back from Oz.

'Yeh, I went to town last week with my mum and I'm officially a **B** cup now,' she said.

I tried not to feel jealous, but as I looked down at my flatter-than-flat chest it was hard not to. You see, I'm still a bit behind everyone else in the puberty stakes. This may be **TMI**, but shall I give you a little update? I mean, we are all friends here, right? So . . .

1. My chest area feels a bit sore, which according to the book my mum bought me means that 'breast growth is imminent' but er hello . . . I'm still waiting!! If anyone is listening, then I'm twelve and a half now so it seems only fair I get some boobs soon.

2. I now have a total of three pubic hairs. Oh, and some kinda fine underarm hair too. I might try shaving it soon, but it seems OK at the mo.

3. I have the dreaded **BO** and I now have to shower **EVERY** day. Oh, how I miss the days when I didn't use to smell. I didn't notice the change much at first, but then Mum started dropping some subtle hints and eventually yep . . . I had to admit she was right.

4. I also have to wash my hair much more
often as it's turned into Grease-ball
Central. I used to get away with washing
it twice a week, but now it's every other
day and even then sometimes it looks as
if I've rubbed it in butter by the morning.
URGH. How is that fair????

5. My skin is deffo oilier too but luckily,
apart from a few small spots, I've
escaped any major breakouts (so far –
touch wood).

6. Period still AWOL. Luckily, it's the same
for Molly and Jess – I wonder who will be
the first?! I just hope I'm not the last.

It wasn't long before the sales assistant started side-
eyeing us and making snooty comments like, 'Are you
actually planning to buy anything, girls?'

I mean, how rude! We'd only been there like two and a
half hours.

I do get that it must be annoying putting away huge amounts of clothes that we were never going to buy, but it's not like she wasn't getting paid for it.

To make a point, Jess bought a pair of sunglasses that were reduced to 99p.

SUNDAY 30 JANUARY

Dead excited right now as Molly starts school tomorrow!
She came round this afternoon to show me her
uniform and check she hadn't made any major fashion
misdemeanours – as if she would!

We made plans to walk to school together tomorrow.
Molly lives the furthest away, so she'll call for me first
and then we'll walk together to pick up Jess, who is
closest.

Then we'll call into the newsagent's and spend our
remaining pocket money on bubblegum to secretly eat in
double science (we sit near the back and Mrs Murphy is
pretty blind anyway).

MONDAY 31 JANUARY

Molly arrived just as I was finishing spooning cereal into my gob. I'd woken up at 8.03 a.m. and had shoved my hair up into a high pony without even brushing it. I hadn't really given my appearance much thought, but as I looked at Molly and then down at my crumpled uniform (would it kill Mum to do some ironing occasionally?!) I suddenly felt very aware.

I tried to point this out to Mum but she didn't seem very keen to take my feedback on board . . .

I don't think I've ever seen anyone make a school uniform look like something you might want to wear for fun, but somehow Molly had. I swear she's got more sass in her little finger than I've got in my entire body.

She had these purply-pinkly moonstone gems in her ears, which looked lovely with her loose orange curls. I'm not sure if I was imagining it, but she even sounded like she had a little bit of an Australian twang in her voice.

'You look great, Mol,' I said.

'Ha. No one looks good in school uniform,' she replied.

'No one except you.'

She rolled her eyes. 'Come on,' she said, threading her arm through mine. 'Let's do this.'

We walked to Jess's house. She was equally excited to see us both.

'The Terrific Threesome,' she said, giggling, as we made

our way to school. 'Kingswood High isn't going to know what's hit 'em!'

In registration Mr Peters introduced Molly and made her stand up and give everyone her interesting fact.

I shuddered, remembering my KitKat Chunky revelation. It still makes me want to die of shame!

It didn't seem to faze Molly though. I mean she's always been more assertive than me, but now she seems to ooze confidence from her pores. I felt a strange mix of pride and a little bit of envy as I listened to her speak.

'My name is Molly. I've just returned from Oz where I was learning to surf and trying unsuccessfully to get a tan (*a few giggles around the room*). I like animals, acting, singing, running, sports and most of all shopping (*more giggles, especially from the girls*). I'm looking forward to getting to know you all. I've been best friends with Lottie since we were five so that makes this all seem a little less scary!'

'That's great, Molly. We are all very much looking forward to getting to know you too, and hearing all about your life Down Under,' replied Mr Peters.

How does she do that?! She absolutely aced it!

Afterwards in the corridor Amber and Poppy came bouncing over to us. I say 'bouncing' as they were literally like a pair of bouncy balls. It immediately made me suspicious.

'Molly, hi!' said Amber. 'It's sooooooo nice to meet you! We've been hearing all about you from Lottie.'

Well, that was a blatant lie!

Just then Beautiful Theo sauntered past and I saw Molly do a double take.

'Is that HIM?!' she said.

I'd already briefed her on Theo and his beautifulness.

'HI, THEO!' called Amber.

'Hi, Amber,' he said, and then, catching my eye, 'Hey, Cucey!'

'Hey,' I replied.

'Did he call you cutie?' asked Molly.

'No, unfortunately, he called me Cucey . . . as in "cucumber".'

'Oh, right . . .' said Molly. But I could tell she wasn't really listening. She was already under Beautiful Theo's spell . . .

Totally besotted

Completely oblivious

TUESDAY 1 FEBRUARY

Daniel smiled and waved to me again today. Molly and Jess are convinced that he likes me. As in not just likes me, but **LIKES ME** likes me. As in I like custard creams, but I **LIKE** KitKat Chunkys.

Maybe I even **LIKE** Daniel more than a KitKat Chunky . . . Maybe I'm in **LOVE** with him?!

What am I even saying? I clearly don't **LOVE** Daniel. I mean, I hardly even know him. I just want to kiss him . . .

OMG, somebody shut me up! **I DO NOT WANT TO KISS DANIEL!** I am only twelve, and the thought of kissing someone scares the life out of me.

What do you even do with your lips? What if you slobber all over your fellow kisser? What if you have bad breath? What if they have bad breath? What if you bash teeth? What if it's a really cold day and your lips get frozen stuck together and you have to call the fire brigade to come and separate you with a crowbar and then the story ends up in the local newspaper?

THOUGHT OF THE DAY:
I am NEVER kissing anybody. EVER.

WEDNESDAY 2 FEBRUARY

All that thinking about kissing Daniel, or, more to the point, NOT kissing Daniel, has clearly made my ability to appear normal in front of him EVEN worse.

This is what happened today . . .

Me and the girls were walking to class after lunch when I saw him and his mates approaching. I tried to play it cool – honestly I did. But it's like this alarm system starts going off inside my head . . .

WARNING WARNING! BOY you Like approaching – don't go all weird!

And then I can see he's just a few metres away. He looks up and our eyes meet. He's coming over! ARGH!!!

Next thing I know he's right in front of me.

He says, 'Hi, Lottie. How are you?'

Inside I'm thinking, *Please act normal, please act normal.*

I make a plan in my brain of how to respond, but by the time it comes out of my mouth the words I want to say have morphed into something that doesn't make any sense AT ALL . . .

Say 'I'm fine, how are you?'

Brine doop

Yes, dear reader, I responded with 'Brine doop'.

He gave me a very strange look and then I did an
awkward laugh and scuttled off to maths.

I mean, **'BRINE DOOP'?!**

What does that even mean???

I tried to cling to the hope that maybe it didn't sound
quite as weird as I thought, but when I turned round
to see Jess and Molly doubled over in fits of giggles I
knew that I had made a serious faux pas. (I learnt that
in French class. It means doing something to embarrass
yourself!)

So, it seems I'm fine smiling and waving at Daniel from a distance, but it's using words that's the problem. And I think it's a pretty big problem because being able to speak to the person you have a crush on is kinda important. So, I'm going to try extra, super hard to be normal around him the next time I see him.

WISH ME LUCK!

THURSDAY 3 FEBRUARY

Since Molly started school, I feel almost like a celebrity by association.

Everybody seems to want to make friends with her, including Amber and Poppy, who are acting all *aren't we super sweet and lovely* again.

I think I prefer it when they are being mean, as at least then I know where I am with them.

Today Amber turned to me, Jess and Molly in registration and said, 'Girls . . . I was thinking . . . maybe we could all meet up for lunch in the canteen one day?'

I WAS LIKE, 'WHAT?!'

'Sure. That would be nice,' replied Molly.

'YAY!' said Poppy. 'We can't wait to get to know you better.'

'Er, hang on a minute,' I said, finding a sudden burst of confidence. 'I thought that we were losers, and you wouldn't want to be seen dead with us?'

'Oh, Lottie, you are so dramatic,' said Amber. 'It was all just LOLS. Right, Poppy?'

'Yep, LOLS!' replied Poppy.

I just stood there with a blank look on my face as they turned and headed off.

'Well, that was weird,' said Jess.

'I know – what on earth are they playing at?' I said. **'LOLS?!'**

'Maybe they feel bad and just want to be friends again?' said Molly.

'I don't think they even know how to feel bad,' I said.

Very, very suspicious.

FRIDAY 4 FEBRUARY

3.47 a.m.

Just had a quite frankly **HORRIFIC** nightmare. Mr Fishy
was back, but this time he had turned mean. I told him
I didn't want to sing with him, but then he tried to force
me to play his weird little guitar. He was very insistent –
it was pretty scary!

I have to admit he did have a point. I'd never thought of it before, but recorders do sound exactly like dying seagulls. I suspect that's why half the parents had their fingers in their ears when my class played 'Rudolph the Red-nosed Reindeer' on the recorder at the Year Four Christmas concert.

4.12 a.m.

Still couldn't sleep. Kept wondering if Mr Fishy was right and maybe I was wasting my life by not exploring my musical talents?!

Went to go and ask Mum and Dad about it and they were incredibly rude!

Apparently Bella had been up for two hours and they had just got her back to sleep, but that's hardly my problem, is it?

4.55 p.m.

I was super late for school this morning (yes, I know – again). I woke up at 8.10 a.m. when I heard Molly ring the doorbell.

'Sorry, Mol,' I said, rubbing the sleep from my eyes. 'I'll have to catch you up.'

Apparently Mum and Dad didn't wake me up because they were so tired that they 'forgot' to set an alarm. Tut, tut – just because they have a baby to deal with now doesn't mean they should neglect their firstborn child. I understand they are struggling with sleep deprivation, but none of this is easy for me either . . . How am I meant to get to school on time if no one comes in to wake me up every five minutes for half an hour?

It's ridiculous. They'll be asking me to make my own breakfast and do my own laundry next! Come to think of it, I have no idea when anyone last bothered to wash my bedsheets, and I even had to get a clean plate out of the dishwasher the other day because no one had bothered to unload it.

Honestly. Does Mum think there is some sort of magic cleaning fairy that comes and deals with it all or something?!

I'd complain to the management, but I know exactly what they'd say – 'Well, why don't you help out around the house a bit more, Lottie?' As if I haven't got enough responsibility in life what with homework, social media management and thinking about boys!

Anyway, I'll stop ranting and get back to the story . . .

When I walked into registration, Amber and Poppy were huddled round Molly, laughing and giggling.

I headed over to Jess, who was completely unfazed and chatting to Meera and Kylie.

'Jess, what's going on over there?' I whispered, side-eyeing them.

'What do you mean? . . . Oh.' She clocked what I was looking at. 'Um . . . they are just chatting . . . right?'

'Just chatting?! Hmm . . . I'm going over.'

I walked across the room. A huge part of me wanted to grab Molly by the arm and drag her away . . .

But I didn't do that because I remembered I wasn't four years old any more.

'Oh, Lottie – hey!' said Amber. 'Molly was just telling us ALL about when you first met. It must be **SO** nice to have been **BEST** friends for **SO** long.' Then she looked at Molly. 'Do you have a matching necklace too?'

'What?' said Molly, looking confused.

'Well . . . I just assumed that seeing as Lottie and Jess have matching necklaces you would have one as well.'

'Oh . . . no . . . I didn't know anything about the necklaces.'

'They are just something me and Jess got each other for Christmas . . . nothing really,' I said, trying to play it down.

'Have you not seen them?! They are two sides of a heart that fit together – you know, like the ones **BEST FRIENDS FOREVER** get.'

Molly smiled but I could tell she was trying not to look bothered. I knew what Amber was trying to do and I wished she would shut up!

Later, after we'd walked Jess home, I said, 'I'm a bit worried you are upset about the necklace thing . . .'

'Nah. I don't need a necklace to prove you are my best friend. I know it in here,' she said, tapping her heart.

PHEW. BIG RELIEF!

SATURDAY 5 FEBRUARY

Spent the morning lounging on the sofa looking at other people's TikToks and wondering how they manage to look effortlessly cool whereas I still appear to be about as cool as a spatula.

what have you got against Spatulas? I mean how else are you meant to get the cake batter out of the bowl?!

There's this move where you have your sunglasses on the top of your head and then you nod your head to a beat and the sunglasses fall exactly into place on your face. Except mine never do. They either fly across the room or land on a sideways wonk. It's so frustrating!

Toby was engrossed in *Minecraft* and I didn't think he was paying me any attention, but then he started giggling and I realized he'd been filming me trying to get the move right.

'Lottie, you are such a **NOOB** at TikTok,' he said, laughing.

'I'm not a **NOOB**! You're a **NOOB**!' I protested, immediately regretting it as the worst thing I can do is pay any attention to him.

'LOTTIE'S A NOOB! LOTTIE'S A NOOB!'

So I put my phone down and proceeded to pummel him with a sofa cushion while he whacked me with a large stuffed orangutan called Kevin.

Mum appeared at the door. 'Hey. What's going on in here? You've woken Bella!'

'Oops,' said Toby.

'Sorry, Mum,' I offered sheepishly.

'Hmmm, you are spending **WAY** too much time staring at screens lately. I think it would be good for you both to have a day off tomorrow.'

'What? That's unfair. You and Dad are ALWAYS looking at your phones, but we never tell you off about it.'

'That's not true!'

'Yes, it is! You spend half your life looking up fantasy houses on Rightmove that we'll never be able to afford.'

'Well, I might do that occasionally, but . . .'

'And Dad's just as bad, always on Twitter looking up funny dog videos.'

'It's hardly constant, Lottie . . .'

'See! There is no way you'd manage a day without your phones, so why should we?'

Mum looked horrified.

In retrospect this was a really idiotic thing to say, because then Mum started going on about how she and

Dad would find it 'incredibly easy' and to prove it she was going to insist upon a technology-free day tomorrow for the **ENTIRE** family.

'NOOOOOOOO, Mum!!!!!!! I need to trade my ultra-rare neon sloth with Luke for his legendary fly-ride albino monkey tomorrow!'

'The mega-ultra neon-flying thingies can wait, Toby!'

I groaned. Simply great.

I guess at least we'll all be suffering together.

SUNDAY 6 FEBRUARY

Woke up this morning and came downstairs. Mum
had been up since 4 a.m. with Bella and decided to
use the extra time to go all out and make a poster and
everything. Clearly she was absolutely loving it!

'Screen-free Sunday – it's got a great ring to it, doesn't
it?' she said.

Errrrr . . . NO.

Apparently we might adopt it as a family policy going forward, as hopefully it'll make us much more present and encourage us to bond and grow as a family.

No one else looked particularly convinced TBH.

Dad made us all bacon butties, which were delish, but we ate in silence.

'I've got a great idea!' said Dad. 'Let's play I Spy.'

I rolled my eyes and Toby groaned. He was undeterred, but it didn't last long . . .

I guess the sarnies were to soften the blow because, after we'd finished, Mum came around with a big Tupperware tub that had a sticky note on the side that said: **Screen Jail**.

Me, Mum and Dad all put our phones in, and Toby's iPad had to be wrestled from his arms. They looked so sad trapped in their plastic prison! It was completely unjust – the poor little guys didn't even know what they had done wrong?!

'Goodbye. I'll miss you. I won't forget you,' I promised.

What a pointless day.

The only things I could think to do involved screens.

Watch YouTube make-up transformations = **screens**

Scroll Instagram/TikTok incessantly = **screens**

Roblox = **screens**

Play *Mario Kart* with Toby = **screens**

Message my friends/call my friends/FaceTime my friends
= **screens**

'I just don't understand what we are meant to do!' I said
to no one in particular.

'Oh, Lottie, there are so many things to do besides staring
at your phone,' said Dad. 'Hopefully this break will
encourage you to use your imagination and think outside
the box.'

I did notice, however, that he kept putting his hand in the jeans pocket where he'd normally keep his phone and then taking his empty hand out and staring at it with a sort of sad look on his face.

(1.07 p.m.)

'I know,' said Mum. 'Let's all go out for a nice walk!'

We all looked out of the window and, as if on cue, a bunch of storm clouds appeared and the heavens opened.

Dad, seeing the horror on our faces, said, 'There is no such thing as bad weather, just bad clothing.'

I said, 'That's the most stupidest saying ever!'

However, everyone in my family is clearly stupid as they were undeterred.

So, dressed in our waterproofs and wellie boots, we all trotted off to enjoy a lovely, delightful walk round the park.

I'm not going to lie: it was horrendous. The only one who

seemed to enjoy it was Bella because she was in her cosy sheepskin-lined pram with a rain cover on. I was super jealous and tempted to try and climb in with her.

After about four million hours Mum finally agreed we'd had enough fresh air and we could go home.

As we walked through the door she said, 'Well, that was lovely. How about we all get nice and dry and snuggle up on the sofa with a hot chocolate and a film?'

'YAY!' said me and Toby.

But then Dad pointed out that the TV was also a screen so that was out of bounds too.

URGH.

3.12 p.m.

Dad suggested doing a jigsaw. What does he think this is? The Victorian era or something?

3.43 p.m.

Completed a twelve-piece Postman Pat jigsaw and an eighteen-piece Paw Patrol one. Did them quite quickly actually. Maybe I'm quite a talented jigsaw do-er.

3.55 p.m.

Just saw that the recommended age range for the jigsaws is three to five. Maybe I'm not a talented jigsaw do-er after all.

UH OH. Mum has set up Snakes and Ladders.

'We all know how Snakes and Ladders ends,' I said, shuddering and pointing at Toby.

'That was ages ago, Lottie. He's grown up a lot since then.'

I was right. First time Toby landed on a snake he rage-quit.

Then, due to all the commotion, Bella started screaming so Mum took her upstairs for a nap.

House dead quiet. Where is everybody? Going to investigate . . .

UNBELIEVABLE!

I went to find my **AWOL** parents and guess where they were . . .

Caught red-handed!

Mum was fully clothed, hiding in the bath looking at million-pound houses on Rightmove, and Dad was under the bed chuckling away at funny dog videos!

I took them back downstairs for a serious chat about their behaviour.

I am thoroughly disappointed in you two!!

'I'm sorry, Lottie. You were right,' said Dad. 'It really is hard to give up screens for an entire day.'

'I hate to say I told you so . . .'

Anyway, the upshot is that Mum announced that our phones had served their time and would be released early for good behaviour. Hurrah!

We all concluded that we had learnt a lot . . .

1. It's best to try and reduce screen time gradually instead of going cold turkey.

2. Quality family-bonding time is massively overrated.

'It's all about moderation,' said Mum.

'Yes, totally,' I said. 'I'll try and cut my YouTube time from three hours a day to two.'

She looked horrified but nodded anyway and we had a lovely evening doing our own version of quality family-bonding time.

5.26 p.m.

DISASTER!

Turned on my phone to discover multiple messages . . .

MOLLY: Just saw your latest TikTok – did you mean to upload it?! Is it meant to be funny?

JESS: Um . . . Interesting TikTok,

Lottie! Is it for real?!?

PANIC!!!

What TikTok?! I hadn't uploaded anything.

I quickly went to the app and opened it up. Somehow in the kerfuffle with Toby I'd managed to upload a video of me trying (and failing) to pull off the sunglasses move culminating with him chanting 'Lottie's a noob!' and trying to attack me with Kevin the orangutan.

The hope that maybe no one had seen it was quickly dashed as I saw the number of views – twenty-five. Including Amber, Poppy, Theo and Daniel.

NOOOO! Why does this sort of stuff always happen to me?

MONDAY 7 FEBRUARY

So today was **TOTALLY HILARIOUS**. Not.

Went into registration this morning and everyone was
sitting there with their sunglasses on their faces like
this . . .

Even Jess had her 99p New Look sunnies on. I mean, call yourself a friend?!? It must have been pre-planned – it's February FGS and the sky is completely grey.

Then I came home to TOTAL carnage. Toby and his friend Leo were running around playing lightsabre battles with kitchen utensils. They'd already broken a vase and a picture frame.

Mum was in the kitchen trying to cook dinner while also jiggling Bella who was screaming her lungs out. She looked like she was about to have a nervous breakdown.

'Can you take her for a minute, please, love?' she said.

'Sure.'

I had no idea how to make babies stop crying, but I tried singing silly made-up songs to her to help calm her down – and what do you know? It worked! She absolutely loved this one (which I made up after she did a huge poop that went all the way up her back) . . .

The whole fam is now referring to me as the Baby Whisperer – not sure if that's a good or bad thing though!

TUESDAY 8 FEBRUARY

Something vaguely interesting to report to you today. Mr Peters made an announcement in registration.

'The school is planning a spring concert after the Easter holidays and there will be various performances by different year groups – music, acting, singing, that sort of thing. I'm sure Mrs Lane will tell you more about it in drama class. I'd love to see a few of your faces up on stage, flying the flag for Seven Green. Right, off to class.'

'Wow!' said Molly, turning to look at me and Jess. 'How cool is that? Shall we all try and take part?'

'For sure,' replied Jess, grinning.

'Um . . . I guess,' I said, knowing that it wasn't really my forte but feeling like I didn't want to get left out. I'll leave the big roles to them and perhaps I can help out backstage. At least that means we'll all get to hang out together.

WEDNESDAY 9 FEBRUARY

Drama today and Mrs Lane revealed that Years Seven and Eight would be getting together to do an abridged performance of *The Little Mermaid*.

Well, I, like, almost wet my pants. I couldn't hold my excitement inside and without thinking I shot up off the carpet where I was sitting, started clapping my hands together and announced . . .

Which was really embarrassing because obviously this is high school and it's not particularly cool to still be into Disney movies. BUT it is brilliant though, right? Closely followed by *Beauty and the Beast*.

Mrs Lane said, 'Well, that's fantastic, Lottie, and I hope to see you at the auditions!'

'I know, Lottie – you could audition for a part as a sea cucumber!' said Amber.

Everyone erupted into laughter. Seriously – was it even that funny?!

Mrs Lane gave Amber a warning look, before continuing, 'Now, the play will consist of performances of the main songs with some short sections of acting in between. It should last about thirty minutes in total so don't worry – there won't be a huge number of lines or lyrics to learn. Does anyone have any questions?'

'OOOH, I do, miss,' said Amber.

Does that girl ever shut up?!??!

'Can I be Ariel? I'm a brilliant singer. You would be able to count on me, miss!'

'That's great, Amber, but you'll have to audition along

with everybody else. I'm sure your enthusiasm, like Lottie's, will serve you well though. Audition details will be available on the drama noticeboard after school.'

Amber's smiled dropped immediately. Did she just expect Mrs Lane to give her the part on the spot?! And anyway I'm sure main parts are much more likely to go to the more experienced Year Eights.

'Any more questions?'

Theo put his hand up.

'Yes, Theo.'

'Can I be the handsome prince?'

Everyone laughed and I noticed that Molly blushed a bit.

Mrs Lane sighed. 'As I said to Amber, Theo, you are welcome to audition alongside everybody else. Right, let's move on. Today we will be warming up by pretending we are very excitable caterpillars who are desperate for the toilet – on your feet, everybody.'   *collective groan*

After school there was a huge crowd around the doors to the drama department. I honestly wouldn't have thought there would be so much interest, but school plays are a bigger deal here than they were at primary school. For a start, there is a proper auditorium with a big stage, curtains and lighting. It all looks very profesh.

Seeing everyone else clamber to get a good look at the audition details did make it feel quite exciting. I'm starting to wonder if maybe I might audition for a proper part after all . . .

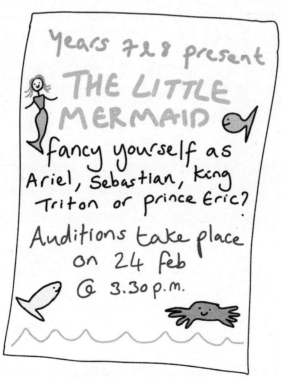

Years 7 & 8 present
THE LITTLE
MERMAID
fancy yourself as
Ariel, Sebastian, King
Triton or prince Eric?
Auditions take place
on 24 feb
@ 3.30 p.m.

When I got home, I told Mum and Dad about the play. They were very glad that I was thinking of auditioning. Toby said he thought I should go for the role of Ursula as we were already terribly similar in looks. Bit harsh! Do I really resemble an evil octopus?!

I resisted the urge to chuck my Müller Corner yoghurt at him. Not because he didn't deserve it but because it was banana with chocolate flakes, which is my absolute favourite – yum!

THURSDAY 10 FEBRUARY

Had after-school detention today for not paying attention in class.

Mr Bishop our geography teacher was ranting on about clouds and I was having a really nice daydream about me and Daniel . . .

We were on our first-ever date and it was going so well! We'd been to the cinema where we shared some popcorn and then we went to Brighton Pier where he won me a humongous cuddly banana on the hoopla. Then we decided to get candyfloss, which was an error because eating candyfloss while holding a humongous cuddly banana turned out to be very messy. Next, we went on the ghost train, again difficult with the banana . . . so I was starting to regret the banana a bit by now, but hey – you live and learn.

Anyway, where was I? Ooooh, the ghost train . . . There were loads of skeletons and zombies jumping out all over the place so it was quite scary! I kept screaming (knowing me, being a bit dramatic on purpose) and Daniel was about to put his arm round me and . . .

Then I heard Mr Bishop shout, **'LOTTIE BROOKS, PLEASE NAME THREE TYPES OF LOW-LEVEL CLOUDS!'**

Wow – how rude was that?! I was just getting to the good part of my daydream too.

Anyway, obviously I'd not been listening to all the boring scientific names for clouds, so I said, 'Errr . . . fluffy . . . wispy . . . and um . . . big?'

The class erupted in laughter, and Jess nudged me and said, 'Good one, Lottie!' which was strange because I wasn't even trying to be funny.

'WRONG! If you had been paying attention then you would know that the answer is stratus, stratocumulus and nimbostratus. So maybe you would like to tell the class why, instead of listening, you have been staring out of the window with a ridiculous look on your face?'

Well, no – I absolutely did not want to tell the class about my date with Daniel and the humongous cuddly banana!

Then Amber decided to say, 'She's probably thinking about the boy she fancies, sir.'

It was a shame I didn't have the humongous cuddly banana to hit her over the head with!

So Mr Bishop says, 'If you are prioritizing boys over learning the scientific names for clouds, then I feel very sorry for you, Lottie, as that's a very sad way to live. You can catch up on everything you have missed in detention after school.'

Ugh, it was so annoying! But the joke was on Mr Bishop because I did not spend my detention catching up on stupid nimbystrimblucumoly cloud names. I spent it daydreaming about Daniel again . . . because he's just so gorgeous and lovely and nice and lovely and . . .

LOTTIE, FOCUS!

Tomorrow is the last day before half-term and I really need to speak to him like a completely normal human, because if I don't it's going to be a **WHOLE NINE DAYS** until I see him again.

FRIDAY 11 FEBRUARY

Amber and Poppy continue to be **SUPER-EXTRA** nice whenever we see them. I keep trying to convince Molly that they are evil incarnate, but it's getting harder by the minute. I mean, today at lunch they let us into the queue in front of them?!

The big downside was that we ended up having to sit with them too.

'**OMG, LOTTIE!** I can't believe it's half-term ALREADY! I mean, it feels like we've HARDLY had a chance to catch up. We are going to MISS you so much!' said Amber.

I was like, 'OMG, yes it's so insane that we've barely spoken seeing as we are **SUCH GREAT FRIENDS!** I'm literally going to go home and cry for, like, the **WHOLE WEEK**.'

Well, that's what I wanted to say, but instead it came out

like, 'Er . . . yeh . . . right.'

'So, we were thinking . . .' said Poppy.

'Sounds dangerous,' retorted Jess.

I sniggered, but Poppy missed the dig entirely and carried on: 'Let's get together over half-term! We could go shopping and maybe grab a Starbucks!'

'Yes,' agreed Amber. 'It'll be just like old times.'

Just like old times?! Slight exaggeration. We've only been to Starbucks with them once. And have they completely forgotten how they tried to turn me and Jess against each other and then completely ditched me as a 'friend'?!

'Sounds fun! I'm in,' said Molly.

Before I had time to say anything, my Daniel radar kicked in.

DANIEL - DAR

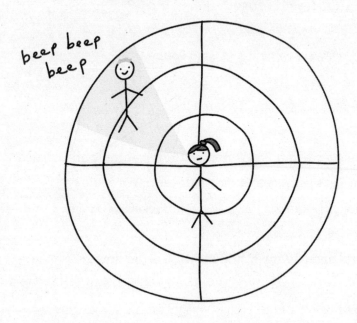

beep beep beep

Sure enough there was Daniel, heading our way. But even though I had seen him I didn't want him to *know* that I had seen him.

Does that make sense??

Suddenly I became very aware of my entire body and didn't know what to do with it. What are you meant to do with your hands when you are a fun, carefree girl having a fun, carefree time with her mates?!

I quickly picked up my packet of Monster Munch with one hand and my can of Fanta with the other, just to give them something to do. They couldn't be trusted to be let loose. I was worried they might start flailing around for no apparent reason.

Annoyingly, at this point, everyone decided to go completely silent. I didn't want Daniel to see us all sitting there like a bunch of boring non-talking people, so I started my (unsuccessful) attempts at casual conversation.

'Has anyone got any good tips on erm . . . how to erm . . . get ketchup stains out of school shirts?'

What was I going on about?! I sounded like my mother.

'Are you OK, Lottie?' asked Molly, giving me a confused look.

'Yes . . . yes . . . I'm totally fine.'

More silence.

I tried again . . . 'Imagine if houses were made from cheese. It would be hard not to eat them, wouldn't it?'

Everyone started looking at me very strangely. Personally, I thought that was a good conversation topic and one I'd like to come back to later.

'Lottie . . . don't look now but Daniel's over there,' said Jess.

I gave her a hard stare as if to say, **DUH! YES, I DO KNOW THAT – THAT IS WHY I'VE GONE ALL WEIRD!**

'In fact, I think he's coming over . . .'

Cue even more silence as everyone sat waiting eagerly to see what would happen. Or more accurately – what an idiot I was about to make of myself.

Come on, I thought. *Help a girl out here!*

More silence . . .

ARGH.

If someone doesn't say something soon, I might be
tempted to come out with my **BRINE DOOP** chat again.
(I think even when I'm like a hundred years old and
sitting in my nursing home, I'm still going to be feeling
awkward about that.)

There was nothing else for it. I adopted an emergency tactic and started laughing manically about nothing.

'That's so funny, Jess!' I said, as I felt Daniel's presence over my right shoulder.

'Hi, Lottie,' he said. 'What's so funny?'

'Oh, we were just laughing at how . . . how . . . erm how . . .'

'We were just laughing at how awkward Lottie gets around boys she likes,' said Amber.

I couldn't believe she said that!

'Oh, right,' said Daniel, blushing. 'Anyway, I just came over to say have a good half-term. Maybe I'll see you around?'

What I should have said here was something like, 'Sure, that'd be great!'

But my mouth said, 'Oh, yeh . . . well . . . I'm, like, really busy and stuff . . . obviously . . . but maybe . . . yeh.'

'Cool. See ya, then,' he replied, looking a bit rejected before walking off.

'Lottie, dude. There is playing it cool and there is playing it cold, and you totally **FROZE** him,' said Jess.

Gah. Why am I such an idiot?! Have I just totally blown it?

SATURDAY 12 FEBRUARY

8.42 a.m.

Seriously, it's the first day of half-term and I'm woken up by Mum hammering on my door.

'Lottie! I'm so sorry to wake you, love, but Bella's really unsettled. Could you try singing her your song?'

So this is my life now. I came up with a really excellent Bella-shushing song and now I'm going to have to sing it to her for eternity. Maybe I should charge Mum? How much do you reckon I'd get? £2 a pop? A fiver if she's desperate?

12.43 p.m.

So even though I obviously know that Valentine's Day is just commercialized nonsense, I can't help but think that it might be the answer to all my problems.

You see, if I can't speak to Daniel and tell him how I feel, then what about if I send him a card instead? Maybe that would make up for my pieing him off yesterday too!

I can't really buy one in the shops as they are all **SO** mushy-gushy, but I could draw him one . . . Is that a really cringe idea or not?! Will it be totally embarrassing, or will he think it's kind of cool? Argh – I don't know.

THOUGHT OF THE AFTERNOON:
Why do people talk about 'pieing' someone off like it's a bad thing . . . Pies are delicious and if someone pied me off I wouldn't mind at all!

In fact I'd open my mouth extra wide so the deliciousness could go directly into my pie hole.

OK, so I've drawn him something . . . What do you think? Shall I give it to him??

I am quite pleased with it, to be honest.

Especially that I remembered that the plural of cactus is cacti – made me sound quite clever. Whether cacti are spunky or not is another matter. I know they are spiky, but that doesn't rhyme with 'chunky' so it was the best I could do.

Inside I wrote:

FROM YOUR SECRET CRUSH X

I did it in big capitals so he wouldn't guess my handwriting, which is probably a bit pointless seeing as my nickname was KitKat Chunky for a large part of the first term, but whatever.

Now I just have to work out how to deliver it to him. I've seen him walking home before, so I know which street he lives on, but I don't know what number.

Lottie the super sleuth needs to put her thinking cap on!

SUNDAY 13 FEBRUARY

Jess came round today and we worked out a solution!
She knows a boy called Liam who lives on Daniel's road
(her mum's an old friend of his mum and he goes to
Kingswood High too) so we decided to WhatsApp him to
covertly extract the deets we needed . . .

> **JESS:** Hey, Liam, hope you are good.
> Just wondering if you knew what
> number Daniel lives at? I need to
> borrow a textbook off him for my
> German homework . . .

> **LIAM:** Hey, Jess, are you feeling OK?! The
> homework isn't due till the end of the
> week . . . and you hate German!

> **JESS:** AU CONTRAIRE, LIAM.
> J'ADORE GERMAN! 🤓

> **LIAM:** Um . . . that's French . . .

JESS: Er, well, yeh . . . that's why I need to get ahead with my homework, duh! So, are you going to tell me what number he lives at or not?

LIAM: Daniel lebt bei number achtundsiebzig.

JESS: YOU WHAT?!

LIAM: 78 😕

JESS: Danke, Herr Liam. Du bist ein entzückender Kätzchen!

LIAM: 'Thank you, Mr Liam. You are an adorable kitten'?!

JESS: Yes. That's exactly what I meant to say 😺

LIAM: Are you flirting with me?!

JESS: I don't know . . . am I?!

LIAM: Du möchtest mit mir
auf ein Date gehen?

Neither of us had any idea what that meant so I quickly
Google-Translated it. 'OMG!!!!!!!! Jess, he's asking you out
on a date!!!!!!!'

'OMG!!!!!!!! WHY?!'

'Maybe because you called him an adorable kitten?!'

'Oh, yeh.'

'Well . . . do you like him?'

'Not as much as I like adorable kittens . . .'

'What shall we do then?'

'Hmm . . . throw my phone out of the window?'

'Great idea!'

(Now listen up, kids . . . throwing your phone out of the
window may *seem* like a good idea at the time BUT it is
highly likely to cause it irreparable damage and get you
into trouble with your parents – especially if you are like
Jess and have shattered your phone screen four times in
the last twelve months.)

Anyway, the upshot is we know where Daniel lives – YAY.
Jess and Molly have agreed to meet me early tomorrow
at 7 a.m. for Operation Lottie Gives Daniel a Valentine's
Day Card **(AKA - Operation LGDVDC)**.

I was too scared to go alone as I don't want to risk being spotted and found out. So, the idea is we are all going to put sporty clothes on and if anyone sees us we are just going to say we are out for an early morning run. How clever are we? Ha!

THOUGHT OF THE DAY:
Maybe I should be a secret agent when I grow up as I feel like I am quite good at being sneaky.

MONDAY 14 FEBRUARY

6.45 a.m.

I don't think I have ever been up this early voluntarily. I
am all dressed in my workout gear. I think it quite suits
me TBH so I might take up being sporty after this.

I read that it is a good idea to spray mystery Valentine's
Day cards with fragrance as smells are highly emotive
and can make feelings feel more feely. Or something like
that. So I went to the bathroom to try and find some of
Mum's perfume. Unfortunately it was still pretty dark so
I fumbled around and sprayed the card with a bottle of
what I thought was Mum's fancy Chanel No. 5.

BIG mistake.

Immediately after spritzing, I inhaled a familiar (not in a
good way) smell and realized my error.

It was not Chanel No. 5. It was 'Poo-Pourri' – a spray that Mum bought for Dad to use to help him cover up the toxic odour of his forty-five-minute pooing sessions. I mean, seriously, why do dads take so long to poo?!

What do they even do in there for so long?! How do their poos stink the entire house out for three hours?!

Still, I had no time to do anything about it now. I only had to hope that Daniel's dad wasn't also a fan of

Poo-Pourri because I didn't want him to open the card
and be immediately reminded of his dad's number-twos.

Right, must dash! The others are here. Wish us luck!

7.45 a.m.

Operation LGDVDC is complete!

It was dead quiet, and nobody saw us at all. Phew. We
just looked like mega-healthy joggers/ninjas enjoying
an early morning run. Molly managed to pop the card
in Daniel's letterbox super quick and then when we
had turned the corner of his road we stopped running
because we realized that running is **HARD**.

Got home and Mum said, 'Well done, Lottie. I think it's
lovely to see you getting up early to exercise – what a
great example you are setting to us all.'

I said, 'Right, yeh well. I did try, but it turns out that
running is actually a bit, I dunno, boring . . . so I might
give it up.'

Then Dad came downstairs and started playing mushy-gushy love songs and dancing around the kitchen with Mum and Bella.

I sat down at the table and waited for his usual 'Oooooooh, Lottie! A mystery card has arrived for you – I wonder who it's from?!' spiel. I mean, it's pretty cringe, but **EVERY** year Dad gets me a card and **EVERY** year I have to pretend I have absolutely no idea who it's from.

So I sat there, waiting . . . and waiting . . . and waiting . . .

Pretty soon I lost my patience and said, 'Are you going to give me my mystery card then or what?!'

He looked dead shocked, then scared and then guilty. I couldn't believe it – **HE'D FORGOTTEN!!!**

I felt pretty deflated, to be honest. I know it's silly, but I didn't realize how much that card meant to me. This is just another example of how I'm becoming sidelined in this family.

To give him some credit, Dad did make me some yummy

heart-shaped pancakes for breakfast with strawberries and cream – but it'll take more than that to get back in my good books!

9.20 a.m.

Have heard nothing from Daniel. Surely, he would have got the card by now??

10.24 a.m.

I guess he could still be asleep though . . .

10.34 a.m.

He must be awake now?? Why hasn't he messaged????

10.44 a.m.

Maybe he's sick? Maybe he's in hospital? Maybe he broke his leg falling down the stairs? Maybe he got bitten by a poisonous snake? Maybe he got attacked by a shark? Maybe he's dead!

10.48 a.m.

It's February so I doubt he went open-water sea swimming, and I don't think we get man-eating sharks in Brighton anyway.

10.51 a.m.

Just googled it and you are more likely to be killed by a cow, a lawnmower or a vending machine than a shark. I didn't realize vending machines were that vicious!

11.01 a.m.

He's probably just still asleep.

11.23 a.m.

If he's still asleep then he is wasting an extremely beautiful day!

Oh God, I sound about forty.

11.44 a.m.

He must be awake by now. It's nearly lunchtime, for goodness' sake!

12.01 p.m.

Dad just came in holding a red envelope! My heart skipped a beat – I dared to hope that it was from Daniel . . .

It was not from Daniel.

It was a very late and very inappropriate card that my father had obviously dashed out to buy from the corner shop.

Now I am **EVEN CROSSER** with him!

Sigh. It's rather pathetic that the only Valentine's Day card I have ever got is from my own father. I wonder what it would be like to get a real one?! I'll probably never find out . . .

OH.

My.

God.

What have I done??

I have just realized that I sent the boy I like a stupid card telling him that I like him more than a KitKat Chunky!

What sort of person does that?!

A complete idiot with marshmallow for brains, that's who!

might actually be quite good as I could eat them out of my earholes – yummy!

WhatsApped the girls.

ME: WHY DID YOU LET ME SEND THAT STUPID CARD?!?! WHY?!!

MOLLY: Lottie, chill. You can just pretend it wasn't you.

JESS: Yeh, I mean how would he ever know?

ME: Well . . . I kind of maybe might have written a little poem on the front.

MOLLY: OK . . . What did the poem say?!

ME: I'm not sure I want to tell you . . .

JESS: Come on, Lottie. How can we help if we don't know what it said?

ME: It said: Roses are red, cacti are spunky . . . I REALLY don't want to say the rest.

MOLLY: Why? That's totally fine so far. I mean it's a bit weird because are cacti actually spunky?! But he deffo wouldn't know it was from you based on that.

JESS: Yeh, he'd just think it was from someone pretty odd?

ME: Erm thanks. The second half is a bit. Well . . . a lot worse though . . .

MOLLY: Go on . . .

JESS: We are waiting . . .

ME: Oh God. OK. So it says . . . Roses are red, cacti are spunky. I like you more than a KitKat Chunky 😬

MOLLY: WHY DID YOU NOT TELL US THIS BEFORE YOU POSTED THE CARD?????

ME: Is it really that bad?!

JESS: It's kind of bad but it's also VERY funny

THOUGHT OF THE DAY:
I should not be trusted to
make decisions by myself.

1.45 p.m.

Amber has posted a photo on Instagram of herself with seven Valentine's cards.

SEVEN!

48 Likes
OMG – 7 V Day cards !!! 😲
Luckygirl # intotalShock
Who are my Secret admirers?!

In comparison I have ONE inappropriate card from a family member. URGH. Not that I'm jealous or anything.

Still heard nothing from Daniel . . . I wish he would put me out of my misery, even if it's just to tell me that he doesn't like me back.

4.22 p.m.

THIS IS EXCRUCIATING.

It's worse than getting into a bathtub of cold baked beans or having 1,000 injections in your toes or drinking an elephant-poo milkshake or having to spend the ENTIRE day doing really difficult algebra problems without a toilet break or EVEN being locked in a wardrobe full of spiders, and also the spiders are really mean and bitey, and also there is a speaker playing 'I Wish It Could Be Christmas Every Day' on repeat even though it's February, and also your phone is out of battery so you can't even play Roblox to pass the time in the bitey-spider wardrobe. Or use the phone to call someone to let you out (which would actually be a better use of the phone if it had battery).

I can't think of any more examples, but you have to trust me – **IT'S REALLY BAD, OK**.

Readers, let this be a lesson to you: if you are tempted to send a Valentine's Day card to a boy you really like and include a **REALLY** bad poem that makes it obvious it's from you, **JUST DON'T**.

6.34 p.m.

There is absolutely no doubt about it – he must have got my **CRINGEFEST** card by now and he's totally ignored it because it's **SO** embarrassing and he feels **SO** awkward. What a total moron I've been.

Please, ground, swallow me up whole!

7.45 p.m.

No, hang on a minute. I am a **STRONG, INDEPENDENT GIRL** and if I want to send a card to a boy I like, then I will. And if he chooses to ignore it, then that's HIS problem. Not mine.

Thank you and goodnight!

THOUGHT OF THE DAY:
Do you think he got the card though? Maybe it got eaten by his dog? Does he even have a dog? Do dogs eat Valentine's Day cards? ARGH.

TUESDAY 15 FEBRUARY

Had a really bad dream.

Woke up all hot and sweaty.

How am I ever going to live this down? How?!

I have come up with an excellent plan. I am not going to go outdoors for the rest of half-term. In fact, I may not even go outdoors for the rest of my life.

I have made a blanket fort like I used to do when I was three. It's quite good, actually – what do you think?

I can just stay in here forever. I have everything I need.

I will allow my family to visit me occasionally and Molly and Jess can FaceTime if they like. But that's it. There will be no other visitors. It's much safer for me to be in a small, enclosed, blankety environment where I can't talk to anyone. If people can't understand that, then that's their problem.

Mum can bring me my meals on a tray . . . that's if I'm able to eat anything, which is unlikely because I am so heartbroken I no longer feel hunger . . . I only feel pain.

The worst thing is that by making that stupid card I have probably tarred KitKat Chunkys for life too. How could I have been so stupid????

2.34 p.m.

False alarm. Briefly left my Fort of Shame to retrieve a KitKat Chunky from the kitchen and it was still very enjoyable, so that's one bit of good news.

3.45 p.m.

OMG OMG OMG OMG!!!

PLOT TWIST!!!!!!!!!!

You will not believe what has happened. I am practically hyperventilating writing this.

Actually, hang on a sec. I need five minutes to compose myself. BRB.

Breathe, Lottie, breathe.

(3.53 p.m.)

Right. So it turns out that Daniel didn't get my card!

You would think this was good news, right? Well, it is, and it isn't.

Because the card somehow ended up with another Daniel . . . Daniel in Seven Blue, to be precise.

Obviously when Jess asked Liam where **REAL** Daniel lived, he must have thought she meant the **OTHER** Daniel.

Get this – they live on the same street. What are the chances?? It must be something like one in a billion to have two people with the same name on the same street!

OK maybe a bit less than that, but, whatever, you get my point.

So, I know what you are thinking . . . How do I know all this?

Well, **OTHER** Daniel posted a photo of the card on his Instagram. He has a private profile, but Amber sent me a screenshot.

This is the caption . . .

Epic V Day card. LOL! Anyone know who has got the hots 4 DAN THE MAN?!?

Guess who the first comment is from??

Yup, my great friend Amber.

'Looks like Lottie B's work to me!' and she even @ed me.

CRINGE!!!

So, there are positives and negatives to this . . .

POSITIVES:

1. **REAL** Daniel didn't get my extremely mortifying card! **BIG BONUS**.

2. **REAL** Daniel therefore does not know that I really like him. Phew (however – see also negatives point 3).

NEGATIVES:

1. I have accidentally declared my love for a guy **I HAVE NEVER SPOKEN A WORD TO**.

2. Thanks to Amber's big mouth it won't be long before the **ENTIRE** school knows.

3. If he hasn't seen it already, it won't be long before **REAL** Daniel also knows, and he will then think that I like **OTHER** Daniel.

4. The guy who I am supposedly in love with calls himself Dan the Man.

5. I think we need to repeat that one – he calls himself **DAN THE MAN!!**

6. I got a nasty paper cut today. Unrelated but worth mentioning as it's really ouchy.

WEDNESDAY 16 FEBRUARY

> **AMBER:** Morning, babe. Hope you don't mind but I gave Dan your digits – he seems pretty keen LOL. Never knew you liked DAN THE MAN 😜

OH MY GOD. I could kill her!

Three minutes later I got a message from DTM.

> **DAN THE MAN:** Wanna share a KitKat Chunky some time?? 😊

I cannot even recall this person even existing so it's very hard to say whether I'd share a KitKat Chunky with him, but, seeing as they are my favourite thing in the ENTIRE world, I'd say it's 99.9 per cent likely to be a firm NO.

Hmmmm. So what do I do? Deny the card was for him? If I do that then everyone would discover that I did actually mean to send it to **MY** Daniel. Well, not **MY** Daniel obviously . . . **BUT** I don't want him thinking that cringe-fest card was for him either.

Would that be worse or better?! **ARGH, I DON'T KNOW**.

Looks like I'll just have to stay hiding in my Fort of Shame a wee while longer.

7.11 p.m.

Everything is spinning wildly out of control!

Apparently me and Dan are now officially 'going out'. It doesn't matter that I don't know who he is – no one is concerned with the details!

I mean, I could walk past him in the street without even knowing. All I've got to go on is a tiny thumbnail Instagram profile pic, but even then it's extra hard to see what he looks like, as for some reason he seems to be wearing a novelty poo-emoji hat (which is quite off-putting TBH).

He has also requested to follow me, but I don't want to accept in case it encourages this strange idea of his that I am his girlfriend . . .

However, I guess he could turn out to be incredibly HOT and that would be good?

THOUGHT OF THE DAY:
If I just ignore the problem, will it magically disappear by the time we go back to school? I'll answer that myself. Yes, it will. Fabulous! All sorted then.

THURSDAY 17 FEBRUARY

I simply CANNOT believe it. Amber has resurrected the
Queens of Seven Green WhatsApp group and added
Molly. **WHY?!** Does she not remember that **TQOSG**
died a grisly death last year when SHE got me into so
much trouble with her **LIES** and **SCHEMING**. How
very dare she!

> **AMBER:** OMG, GIRLS!!!! It's been SO long! I
> know we had a few misunderstandings last
> year, but it'd be great to put all that behind
> us. So, I was wondering if you fancied
> coming over to mine tomorrow? We can just
> chillax and catch up – it will be SO much
> fun! xx

Yeh right. It'll be about as much fun as getting a tooth
removed at the dentist, if the dentist was a gorilla using
a sledgehammer!

Anyway, I looked at the message in disbelief and then immediately WhatsApped Molly and Jess.

ME: ERRRRRRR, WHY ON EARTH WOULD WE WANT TO GO OVER TO HER HOUSE?!?

JESS: Seems a bit weird, right? What is she playing at?

MOLLY: Well . . . Maybe she is actually sorry? It was probably hard for her to apologize and she's been so kind and friendly to me since I joined Kingswood. Maybe you could give her another chance?

WHAT?!?!?!

JESS: I guess Molly has a point, she has been much nicer lately . . . Plus I'm not being shallow but I hear she lives in one of those massive houses down by the seafront and that her parents are LOADED . . .

WHAT?!!?!?

Was I the only one who could see what was happening here? My two friends were being completely sucked in.

I wasn't falling for it at all, but I also didn't want to be the one causing problems. I needed to be the mature person here and consider giving her another chance (and yeh . . . if I'm totally honest I was kind of intrigued to check out her massive house too).

ME: I mean, I guess we could go for a little bit, but if they start getting annoying then we need a secret signal so we can all leave, right? Maybe pull on your right earlobe three times

JESS: Deal!

MOLLY: Double deal!

FRIDAY 18 FEBRUARY

Tried on three different outfits but they all look awful.

I shouted down to Mum, **'I HAVE NOTHING TO WEAR!!!!!!!!!!!'**

She shouted back, 'You have loads of things to wear, Lottie!'

'No, I don't. I have **LITERALLY** nothing **AT ALL** to wear.'

'You need to look up the meaning of the word "literally" because if you take it in its true sense then you would have zero items of clothing and would therefore be walking around completely naked.'

Why do parents always have to be so annoying?!

'FINE! I HAVE LITERALLY NOTHING COOL TO WEAR!'

'CAN EVERYONE STOP SHOUTING ACROSS THE HOUSE, PLEASE!' said Dad. While also shouting across the house.

Settled on an inoffensive choice of jeans, trainers, T-shirt and black bomber jacket.

Made a mental note to get my ears pierced. A good way to make boring outfits look a bit edgier. Just need to get over my needle phobia first.

(6.23 p.m.)

You would not believe Amber's house!

First, think of the nicest house you've ever been to . . . Have you got a picture of it in your head? Right, now times that by ten. No wait – times that by 100! Now you might have something close to Amber's house.

Basically, it's **HUGE!** Also, it's super posh. Her dad has a Porsche in the driveway. Insane, huh? I've never known a real-life person with a sports car. We have a Ford Focus along with ninety-five per cent of the population.

She was home alone when we arrived. Apparently her mum and dad work really long hours for some sort of bank so they aren't often around. Amber said one big advantage of having parents who work long hours is that they buy you loads of clothes and make-up because they feel guilty about not being there. I wish my mum and dad would work longer hours. My house is so loud and noisy I can barely think.

Make-up

Amber told us that when she was younger she used to have live-in nannies, but after the last one left her parents decided she was old enough to be left alone so they didn't get a replacement. Now during the holidays she has the house to herself, which is great because she can do whatever she likes, whenever she wants. Amazing.

First, she gave us a tour of the house and we were all like **'ooooooh'** and **'ahhhhh'** the whole way round. The kitchen was all white and shiny and the fridge was like one of those massive American ones you see on *Cribs* with an ice maker on the front. She had, get this, a room that she called 'the snug' but it was actually a cinema room with a proper massive screen and big lounge chairs and beanbags.

Next, we went upstairs, and she showed us her bedroom. She had a giant bed! Not even a double but a king-size – imagine having a king-size bed when you are eleven! Insane.

Everything was sooooo stylish with lots of grey, pink and velvet. One entire wall of her room was made up of wardrobes and she had a dressing table full of lovely-looking perfumes and body sprays. There is no way she'd have ended up accidentally spraying a Valentine's Day card to the boy she liked with her dad's Poo-Pourri.

The bedroom tour didn't stop there because she has her own en-suite with a roll-top bath like you see in movies and magazines. Plus a walk-in shower and the fluffiest pink towels you ever saw!

I won't lie. I felt pretty jealous. It was hard not to be. I kept remembering the times she visited my house and feeling quite embarrassed. I wonder what she thought of it . . . my single bed with unicorn bedcovers, the embarrassing Justin Bieber memorabilia everywhere, and hamster food and sawdust spilling out all over the tattered beige carpet.

I also have to share a bathroom with my entire family! It's full of kids' toys and squeezy soap and magic colour-change bubble bath. It's not relaxing at all. If I had a bath like Amber's, I'd probably wallow in it for hours, but I tend to take a shower these days as it's quicker. Plus don't even talk to me about the toilet – as if Dad's poo sessions weren't bad enough, Toby never bothers to put the toilet seat up, so nine times out of ten when I go in after him it's covered in little-boy pee – gross!

After we'd finished the tour we went back to the kitchen and Amber made us cocktails in proper fancy cocktail glasses that you get in hotel bars. She added blended watermelon to the glass and then topped it up with pineapple juice and pink lemonade. Then she added lime slices and those miniature mouse umbrellas as garnishes. It was **SO** delicious.

w big mouthfuls and started feeling a bit
...nd funny in the head. Then I fell over absolutely
no...ing and threw the rest of my drink across
the floor . . .

Everyone laughed at me because apparently 'mocktails'
don't contain any actual alcohol. What an idiot!

If I'm that giddy and clumsy when I'm not drunk,
just imagine what I'd be like if I was drunk! I shudder
to think . . .

Next, Poppy said, 'Amber, could we go in the hot tub?'

Me, Jess and Molly were like, 'Hot tub? No way!'

None of us had our swimmers, but Amber said that was
fine because we could borrow some of hers. We went
back to her room and she opened up a drawer that was
bursting full of bikinis and swimsuits.

'Take whatever you like!' she said casually, and all the
girls immediately started rifling through her collection,
picking their favourites. I chose a sporty-looking one
with a crop top rather than one of those triangle-shaped
string things. I don't feel very comfortable wearing
anything too revealing.

I was a bit embarrassed getting changed in front of
everyone else. But Amber didn't seem to care so I felt
silly suggesting I'd like to go and get changed in private.
It's shockingly unfair when you think that I'm the eldest
out of all five of us girls but I still have the smallest
boobs. Mum says, 'Everything happens in good time,'
but that's just one of those silly sayings that people use
when they don't have anything helpful to say.

I put my bikini on as quickly as possible while facing into a corner and reminded myself that no one else would be thinking about the way I looked. It's always all in your head, right?

Amber took the cover off the tub and switched on the bubbles. It wasn't even one of those blow-up ones but a fancy one with proper seats and pink and purple lights. Apparently it's for eight people, but once she managed to fit fifteen friends in.

I wish I had a hot tub and I also wish I had fifteen friends to put in it!

Inevitably the conversation turned to the subject I'd been most dreading. 'So, what's going on with you and *Dan the Man*, Lottie?' asked Amber. She was trying to keep a straight face (and failing).

I couldn't deny that I'd sent him the card because then they'd know the truth. So I said, 'Oh, nothing. It was just a joke more than anything.'

'It did seem kind of weird, because I always thought you liked Daniel and not Dan,' said Poppy.

'Me too,' Amber agreed, 'but that's good because I hear that Marnie is really into Daniel . . . and she's planning to ask him out.'

I hoped I managed to pull off a fake smile because inside I felt like someone just shot an arrow through my heart. I imagine, if that had happened for real, the only thing Amber would care about was me making a mess of the hot tub.

Lottie please could you try not to bleed in my hot tub!

Why is she constantly trying to say stuff that she knows will hurt me and how does she always manage to do it in a way so that no one else really notices?

Suddenly I started to feel out of place so I decided to initiate the secret signal.

Jess noticed right away, but Molly seemed completely transfixed by Amber and Poppy. I must have pulled my earlobe like twenty-seven times – I probably nearly pulled it clean off.

oops. I think I needed that...

We ended up leaving without her and I couldn't help but feel quite down about it. It was clear that Amber was more interested in impressing Molly than us.

'I mean, she does have an amazing house, but that doesn't give her the right to laugh at people . . .'
I said to Jess as we walked home.

'Yeh, I guess. But maybe you have to think about why she behaves like that . . . She's probably pretty lonely . . . It can't be easy being on your own all the time.'

'I suppose, but that doesn't make it OK to be mean . . .'

'No, it doesn't. But it makes me understand her a bit better . . . Right, come on,' she said, sprinting off down the road. 'Last one to yours is a pair of Toby's smelly pants!'

I laughed and started to run after her, knowing I'd never catch up – I'm so lucky to have a friend like her, no matter that she always tries to see the best in people.

Later on when I was back with my very average family in my very average house, I told Mum and Dad that I spent the day drinking mocktails in a hot tub. I also told them that it would be good if they could work a bit harder to afford us a better lifestyle in which I could have my own roll-top bath and approximately eighty-three different pieces of swimwear.

I don't think that was too much to ask, but they just laughed. How rude.

RECURRING THOUGHT OF THE DAY: I know technically nothing has happened with me and Daniel, but I thought he liked me and I REALLY like him. I hope this thing about Marnie asking him out is fake news.

SATURDAY 19 FEBRUARY

Picture the scene. Whole family sitting down eating Mum's speciality beef stew. Boke.

Toby announces out of nowhere: 'Lottie's got a boyfriend.'

'**WHAT?!** No, I have not!' I said.

'Yes, you have. Millie's big sister Lucy told her . . . then she told Bethany, and Bethany told Leo, and Leo told me!'

I stared blank-faced. What was happening?! Even the local primary schools seemed to know about it!

'Well, there's no need to be so secretive, Lottie. That's great news! What's his name?' said Dad.

I was unable to comprehend what was actually going on . . .

'His name is **DAN!**' Toby laughed.

'OOH Dan! Lovely name,' said Mum.

'LOTTIE AND DAN, SITTING IN A TREE, K.I.S.S.I.N.G.!'

'I've not got a boyfriend! I've never even met Dan!'

'Well, if you've never even met him, then how is he your boyfriend?' asked Dad.

'Exactly! He's not my boyfriend! He just thinks he is due to an . . . admin error . . .'

'A what?!' said Mum.

'It's a long story.'

One that I **REALLY** didn't want to have to explain to my **ENTIRE** family! Why can't I seem to get through to people?

THOUGHT OF THE DAY:
Is it really that cruel to dump someone by WhatsApp if you've never even met them? What about doing it via a TikTok dance routine?

SUNDAY 20 FEBRUARY

9.34 a.m.

I woke up feeling anxious at the thought of going back to school tomorrow and facing Dan **AND** Daniel. I needed some advice from someone with more boy experience than me, so I texted my ultra-cool next-door neighbour Liv. She's fourteen and has had approximately 137 boyfriends so far – impressive, right?

> **ME:** HELP! I have accidentally got myself a boyfriend that I've never met. What do I do?!

> **LIV:** Errr . . . how did you accidentally get a boyfriend? Did you trip up and fall over on top of him or something?!

ME: No, I sent a Valentine's Day card to him . . . but it wasn't meant for him. It was meant for another boy also called Daniel . . . but I can't tell him that because I don't want him to know that I wrote him a poem declaring that I liked him more than a KitKat Chunky.

LIV: ?!?!? How on earth do you get yourself into such ridiculous situations, Lottie??

ME: I honestly don't know. What do I do??

LIV: Well, firstly . . . is the new Daniel guy nice?

ME: I doubt he's as nice as a KitKat Chunky . . .

LIV: No boys are as nice as chocolate – that's scientifically impossible. However, maybe give him a chance . . . He might actually be hot! But if you don't like him like that, then I'd tell him straight away. My advice would be to do it quickly – like ripping a plaster off.

ME: OK thanks, Liv. Wish me luck!

LIV: Good luck xx

3.11 p.m.

DAN: 'Hey Hun. Wanna meet for lunch tomorrow? X'

Hun? **HUN?!?!** Why is he calling me hun???

I have a really bad feeling about this, but I need to let him down as soon as possible so I just replied saying:

ME: OK. See you by the sports hall at 12.15 p.m.

I felt a bit mean not adding an **X** in return, but I really don't want to encourage the guy. Best keep it business-like for now.

THOUGHT OF THE DAY:
Oh God, what have I done?!? Last week I'd barely even spoken to a boy, and now here I am about to dump one! I never knew I would be such a heartbreaker.

MONDAY 2I FEBRUARY

So today I met my 'boyfriend' for the first time.

All I knew about him was that he had brown hair (which describes about eighty per cent of the boys at school) so I was quite scared that I'd turn up and I wouldn't even know who he was. I had guessed he was pretty tall though, going by his nickname.

Luckily, he knew what I looked like so after I'd been standing there like a doughnut for a few minutes I felt someone tug the arm of my blazer. And that was my very first glimpse of Dan.

I had to look down as he only came up to my shoulder! I was immediately confused . . .

I took a deep breath and said, 'Dan, look, I'm sorry but I don't think this is going to work . . . It's all moved a bit too quickly and to be honest I'm not sure we are compatible.'

Dan looked like he was about to cry and said, 'Is it because of my height? I'm due a growth spurt any day now, so I'll probably be getting taller soon.'

It was a bit, but I didn't want to make him feel bad.

'No, it's not that, Dan.'

'Even if I don't get taller, it doesn't really matter. You could just bend down when we kiss, or I could stand on a wall or a chair? My mum's got one of those portable stools with the fold-out legs that she uses to get things out of the high-up kitchen cupboards – I could bring it with me on dates?'

NO!!!

This was not going well at all.

I did not want to be thinking about Dan the Man kissing me. And I most certainly did not want to be thinking about Dan the Man puckering up to kiss me using his mum's portable kitchen stool!

. . . Also, what would Dan the Man's mum do if me and Dan were out on a date (with the stool) and she urgently needed to get a can of beans out of a high-up cupboard? Maybe they'd have to work out a rota or something?

Then I thought – **LOTTIE, FOCUS!** No one ever urgently needs to get cans of beans out of high-up cupboards.

Anyway . . . back to the story . . .

I realized this was going to be more difficult than I had hoped. I needed to stop him talking, I needed to tell him we were **OVER**.

I remembered what Liv said. I had to give it to him straight.

'Dan. Listen. It's not your height, I promise. Unfortunately, I kind of like someone else . . .'

Then the worst thing happened. He started crying. I was mortified . . . I'd only said about three sentences to him ever. What was he crying about?!

'I'm sorry for getting emotional. It's just I really liked you, Lottie,' he said through his sobs.

'I like you too. It's just that the timing is all wrong. Maybe in a few years' time when you are a bit taller. I MEAN, OLDER . . .'

That didn't help so I begrudgingly offered him my packet of Monster Munch. It seemed to soften the blow a bit . . .

For him anyway. I was really looking forward to those.

As I left to meet the girls, I caught **REAL** Daniel's eye. He was standing with a group of friends a few metres away. He looked down quickly, but I know he must have seen me and Dan the Man together.

I really wanted to explain to him that there is nothing going on between us and in actual fact I was just dumping Dan the Man. But how do I do that when I can't formulate sentences around him?

10.34 p.m.

Urgh. I don't think I'm going to be able to sleep tonight. Every time I close my eyes, I picture Dan the Man standing on his mum's portable kitchen step making a goldfish face at me.

TUESDAY 22 FEBRUARY

People kept coming up to me in school today and saying how sorry they were to hear about me and Dan the Man – for crying out loud, we'd only been 'going out' for a week!

It didn't help that he was in the canteen causing a scene at lunchtime by sobbing into his lasagne and chips. I think I had a lucky escape there. Imagine what he'd have been like if we'd been actual boyfriend and girlfriend!

Slightly overdramatic!!

Whenever I see Daniel, he looks away and avoids me. He must think I do/did actually really like Dan the Man, but he's got it so wrong and I have no idea how to fix it.

Luckily, most people seem to be more interested in discussing the play, because auditions are in two days – **EEK!!**

About fifty per cent of the girls in Years Seven and Eight are going for the part of Ariel. It's going to be cut-throat out there, I tell you. Amber seems to think that she has it in the bag, and Molly is trying to play it cool, but I can see her heart is set on it too.

I know it's mean, but I really, really hope that Amber doesn't get it. I just can't stand her being so arrogant about it all.

Jess is, as usual, dead casual about the whole thing and happy to play any part she's given. Secretly though I think she's hoping to bag Flounder as he's her absolute fave. As for me, I'd be delighted to get into the chorus because being in the spotlight isn't really my thing (at least, not on purpose).

WEDNESDAY 23 FEBRUARY

Spent about two hours practising my audition piece
using the old hairbrush-in-the-mirror technique. We
have to choose one of the Little Mermaid songs to sing and
most people are doing 'Part of Your World'. I've decided
to do 'Under the Sea' because it's more of a comedy
performance and easier to hit the notes. I already
know all the words by heart, thanks to a bordering-on-
unhealthy Disney obsession between the ages of four
and eight (possibly ten and a half, if I'm honest).

I thought I sounded quite good, but Toby kept shouting
stuff like, 'DAD, CAN YOU TELL LOTTIE TO SHUT UP?!
SHE SOUNDS LIKE A SHEEP WHO HAS JUST BEEN
PUNCHED IN THE FACE BY A BADGER!'

So I shouted back, 'DAD, CAN YOU TELL TOBY THAT HE'S
AN IDIOT AND THAT BADGERS DON'T GO AROUND
PUNCHING SHEEP?!'

'DAD, CAN YOU TELL LOTTIE THAT SHE'S ACTUALLY
THE IDIOT BECAUSE I SAW A BADGER PUNCH A SHEEP

ON YOUTUBE ONCE AND THAT'S EXACTLY WHAT SHE
SOUNDS LIKE WHEN SHE SINGS?!'

'DAD, CAN YOU ASK TOBY TO EXPLAIN WHY ON EARTH
A BADGER WOULD EVER PUNCH A SHEEP?!'

'MAYBE THE SHEEP SCRATCHED THE BADGER'S CAR AND
THEN TRIED TO RUN AWAY LIKE THAT GUY WE SAW IN
TESCO'S CAR PARK LAST WEEK!'

'DAD, I CAN'T LIVE WITH THIS MORON ANY MORE –
HE'S ROTTING MY BRAIN CELLS! CAN WE SELL HIM TO
THE CIRCUS?'

Dad shouted back, 'CAN YOU BOTH BE QUIET?! I'M
FINDING IT VERY DIFFICULT TO CONCENTRATE ON MY
FUNNY DOG VIDEOS!'

Then Mum shouted, 'I'M TRYING TO GET BELLA TO SLEEP.
IF YOU DON'T ALL SHUT UP RIGHT NOW I'M GOING TO
(insert rude language).'

Just another happy, functional day in the Brooks household!

THURSDAY 24 FEBRUARY

7.13 a.m.

EEEEK, up pretty early to wash my hair so that I look nice(ish) for the audition. I can't believe I'm actually going to do this. I can't believe I'm going to voluntarily put myself up on a stage and sing in front of actual people! It seems utterly mad, but I'm going to be brave and put myself out there because I'm determined not to be that shy girl who never tries anything for fear of failing.

My hamsters are being super supportive as usual. (Well more so Prof. Squeakington. Fuzzball looks half asleep.) Every time I doubt myself, I'm going to think of them and how they always have my back.

OMG, I DID IT!

First, Mrs Lane gathered us together and said that she was aware of the large amount of interest in the role of Ariel, but that there are lots of other great parts up for grabs too, so not to be disheartened if you don't get it . . . blah blah blah, etc. It's obvious there is going to be a huge drama when the cast list gets revealed.

Then we all had to line up outside the drama department and she started calling people in to audition, one by one. Most people sounded great and as the queue got smaller and smaller I got more and more nervous. I had to go to the toilet more times than I would like to say, as I kept thinking I might pee my pants!

Amber was two spots ahead of me and she was still telling everyone within a three-mile radius how amazing she was going to be as Ariel. I couldn't believe how confident she was!

When it was her turn to go in, we all stopped talking and went super quiet as we were very intrigued to hear what her 'amazing voice' sounded like. Weirdly though, she really didn't sound very good at all – she was completely off-key. I may have to apologize to Toby because perhaps

his analogy did make sense after all – she sounded just
like a sheep being punched in the face by a badger!

Everyone in the queue looked at each other as if to
say, *Eh?!*

She didn't seem to realize how bad she had sounded
though, as she looked dead chuffed with herself when she
came out. In fact, she was positively beaming.

'How did it go?' asked Jess.

'Fab! Mrs Lane pretty much said I have the part in the bag.'

WHAT?! Did she even hear herself?!

She was like one of those *X-Factor* contestants who go and audition thinking they are the bee's knees, even though they can't sing at all, just because their families told them they could.

Molly was next, and she sounded great, but annoyingly she forgot her lyrics and had to start again. I told her not to worry and that it didn't matter, but I think she was really cross with herself.

Then it was me! I felt the butterflies in my tummy and my heart started to beat super-fast. I remembered what Mum told me about taking deep breaths and closing my eyes to try and calm the panicky feeling. Then I walked to the middle of the stage and looked at Mrs Lane – she was sitting what seemed liked miles away in the middle of the auditorium with another drama teacher, Mr Coombes, and two older kids from Year Ten who would be helping with the production.

'Hi, Lottie. How are you feeling?' she said.

'I'm OK. A bit nervous,' I replied.

'A bit of nerves is fine; they can actually help. But take your time and start when you are ready.'

And so I did it. I thought it went OK – I didn't freeze up and I remembered all the words but, apart from that, I couldn't really say how it sounded. It was only when I walked back out into the hallway and people kept saying stuff like, 'Oh wow – Lottie, you can really sing!' that I realized that maybe I'd done an OK job after all. I was dead shocked, but also pretty pleased.

Jess went in next, and she sounded incredible! Like it was just so effortless. The entire line gave her a round of applause when she came out.

When everyone was done, Mrs Lane came back out and thanked us all for coming. She told us we would find out our parts next Wednesday when they would be pinned to the drama department noticeboard. She also told us not to be disappointed if we didn't get a main singing part because there was always next time and she needed plenty of extras in the chorus and to help behind the scenes too.

When we walked home, me and Jess were on cloud nine, absolutely buzzing from the audition. It was such a big deal for me as I would have **NEVER** had the guts to do this kind of thing before.

Molly looked kind of sad about the whole thing though. I think she was beating herself up about forgetting her lyrics. We tried to tell her it didn't matter, but I'm not sure it worked.

FRIDAY 25 FEBRUARY

Who in their right mind decides to have babies?! I mean, honestly – Bella screamed **ALL NIGHT LONG!**

Mum said it was either colic or teething or indigestion or wind or developmental leap (whatever that means) . . .
I thought maybe it was just 'being an annoying little sister'?!

I could barely function at school today. I had **HUGE** bags under my eyes – in fact they were so big they were practically suitcases.

By my sixth-period history class I was so tired that I fell asleep on my desk. Apparently I was out for about fifteen minutes before Mr Simmonds woke me up by shouting, **'LOTTIE BROOKS, HOW YOU CAN SLEEP THROUGH THE INDUSTRIAL REVOLUTION I'LL NEVER KNOW!'**

Unfortunately, I was very shocked and confused – and committed the ultimate faux pas of calling a teacher Mummy, which FYI is even worse when the teacher is a man.

Even more unfortunately the class seemed to think I'd said it as a joke, so now I have to write a 1,500-word essay on 'How Britain became a modernized country'. Cheers for that, Bella!!!

Still, it was nice to see Nigel the blob of drool all over my history book. I'd missed him!

SATURDAY 26 FEBRUARY

Just got back from town with the girls and I have the most exciting news to tell you. It's even more exciting than when I discovered strawberry frappa-whappa-dingdongs (I still can't remember the proper way to say it). Anyway . . . today I had my first bubble tea and **OMG!!!!!!!!!!**

You must have one now. I mean it. Stop what you are doing, do not pass go, do not collect £200 – just go to your nearest bubble-tea shop and order one. If you aren't old enough to go into town on your own, then get down on your hands and knees and beg your mum or dad to take you. Seriously, blame me – say Lottie told you, you **NEED** one **ASAP**.

So here's how it works . . . you go into the bubble-tea shop and you can choose any flavour of tea you like and, when I say 'tea', it's not like the boring tea your parents drink – it's basically juice and then you can get any flavour of bubbles! I had white peach with passionfruit and blueberry popping boba (popping boba is a type of bubble that bursts in your mouth – it's a taste sensation!).

Jess chose apple fruit tea with strawberry and kiwi popping boba and Molly got raspberry with lychee and cherry popping boba. We tried each other's and although they were all good I liked mine the best, which was great because I **HATE** it when you make a bad choice and you are jealous of everyone else's.

I think when I'm older I might open my own shop called Lottie's Bubble Tea! Imagine how much fun it would be. I could just sit around drinking bubble tea all day long.

Anyway, me and Jess and Molly were sitting there drinking our teas and guess who we see walking past the window. Uh huh, Beautiful Theo and **REAL** Daniel.

On instinct I just ducked under the table to avoid being seen.

'What on earth are you doing, Lottie?' asked Jess.

'Oh, um . . . I dropped an earring!'

'Errr . . . you don't have your ears pierced,' said Molly.

I pointed discreetly at the boys through the window. 'I don't want him to see me. I'm scared I'll do something stupid.'

'What's more stupid than hiding under the table looking for a non-existent earring?' Jess said, laughing.

'Exactly.'

I crawled out when the coast was clear and noticed

Molly was still staring dreamily through the window in the direction the boys had headed.

'You'd better watch out,' I said to her after they'd gone. 'You know Amber will kill you if you get together with Theo, right?'

'What makes you think I like Theo?' she asked.

Oh, how we laughed!

SUNDAY 27 FEBRUARY

I keep thinking about Daniel and I really don't know what to do.

Does he think that I like/liked Dan the Man?

Is that why he's avoiding me at school?

Does he still like me?

Did he ever really like me?!

Has Marnie asked him out?

Would he say yes if she did?

Has he seen that awful Valentine's Day card?

What colour are his eyes if you look into them really close up?

What would it feel like to hold his hand?

Will I ever be able to speak to him like a normal human?

What came first: orange the fruit or orange the colour?

How can people tell you they are speechless if they are actually speechless?

Do fish get thirsty?

Can you die in the living room?

What if you want to stand up in the sitting room?

In the cinema how do you decide which arm rest is yours?

Is the word 'dictionary' in the dictionary?

Is a fly without wings a walk?

What do you call a female daddy-long-legs?

What do you call a male ladybird?

Do penguins have knees?!?

So many questions, so few answers!

I guess the only way to find out is to come clean and
admit to Daniel that I like him and that I sent him the
most cringetastic card in the entire world. I'm going to
have to put my big-girl pants on and do it.

MONDAY 28 FEBRUARY

I did mean to try to speak to Daniel today, but when I saw
him in the corridor I just froze, like, literally, against the
wall like a rabbit in the headlights, as my dad would say.

Mr Peters was also walking down the corridor and when
he saw me he got a concerned look on his face and said,
'Is everything OK, Lottie? You seem a little distant lately.
Why don't you go to the office and ask to have a chat to
the school counsellor?'

I said I was absolutely fine and went off to RE. I wonder
if the school counsellor does have any advice on how to
talk to boys though?

TUESDAY 1 MARCH

ARGH, BIG DAY TOMORROW!!! We find out the parts
we will have for the play. The whole of Years Seven and
Eight are buzzing about it so it feels dead exciting.

We are guaranteed to get some sort of part so I'm not
that nervous. To be honest, the smaller the better for me
as then I won't be spending the next six weeks stressing
out about it all. Behind the scenes would be OK too.
Maybe I can do hair and make-up or something?!

I think I'm more nervous for Molly! She will be devo if
Amber gets Ariel and vice versa.

WEDNESDAY 2 MARCH

BLIMMIN' ECK! You won't believe what happened today. I'll start from the beginning . . .

I met up with Molly and Jess on the way into school as usual. We agreed to arrive early for once as we knew Mrs Lane was putting up the cast list first thing.

It was really strange pushing our way to the front of the crowd to get a squiz at the list – there were people celebrating, people crying, people almost getting trampled to death on the floor. I felt a bit like I was in some sort of American high-school movie!

My eyes automatically went to the bottom of the list as I expected to be in the chorus at best. When I didn't find my name there, I started working my way up . . .

And up . . .

And up . . .

I could not believe it! I had got the part of Sebastian!

'Congrats, guys,' I heard Molly say sadly.

'What?! . . . What did you get?' I asked, my eyes scanning the list. That's when I saw who got the part of Ariel . . .

'OMG – JESS!'

She was standing there, staring at her name and looking like she was about to faint.

At that moment, Amber elbowed us out of the way. Her face turned from a smug satisfied grin to pure rage.

'RIDICULOUS! They wouldn't know talent if it came round and whacked them right in the face!'

What was going on? I scanned the list again and saw Molly, Poppy and Amber's names in the chorus section as 'generic fish'. Ouch.

In some weird twist of fate the two main contenders for the star role had been cast in the chorus and the two people who would have been more than happy being in the chorus had been cast in big roles.

'I'm really sorry, Molly,' said Jess as she placed a sympathetic arm round her shoulder.

'Me too,' I said, and I meant it.

'It's OK, guys. You were both great and you totally deserve it.'

I could tell how disappointed she was, and it must have been hard to see me and Jess get the news she was so desperately hoping for.

When I got home, I told Mum and Dad the news and they were absolutely thrilled. I can't work out how I feel though . . . Pleased? . . . Terrified? A mix of both, probably. I mean, I've got to dress up as a blimmin' crab!

This is a really **BIG** deal for me and I'm not really sure I have the confidence to pull it off. I'm going to try my absolute hardest though.

THURSDAY 3 MARCH

Daniel walked past me in the lunch queue today and said, 'Congrats on the Sebastian gig, Lottie!'

And I said, 'Thanks, I've always dreamt of being a singing crustacean.'

'A what?'

'A crustacean . . . is an um . . . a term used to describe creatures that live in water and have a hard outer shell . . . Lobsters and shrimps are other examples . . .'

Even while I was saying it, I was thinking, *Why am I talking like I'm a dictionary?!*

'Oh right, well, that's interesting to know . . . Congrats on the singing-crustacean gig then.'

'Yeh. Thanks.'

I then proceeded to my locker. I opened it, placed my head in as far as it would go, and then I did a big silent scream.

Why am I like this?!?

However, the one positive is that Daniel is now being friendly with me again! Maybe there is still a chance for us after all?!

FRIDAY 4 MARCH

Things have been a bit weird.

Molly is still clearly down about the play but keeps saying she's fine. Me and Jess are trying not to talk about it too much in front of her, but at the same time there isn't that much else to talk about. I feel really guilty about it, even though I know it's not my fault.

Meanwhile Amber is going around telling anyone who will listen that she 'was robbed' and threatening to take legal action against the school. I mean, imagine trying to sue the school because you didn't get the part you wanted in a play?! Ridiculous.

SATURDAY 5 MARCH

Decided to text Liv about the Daniel dilemma.

> **ME:** Help. I can't talk to boys!
> Or more specifically the boy I like.
> As in LIKE like! 😍

> **LIV:** Don't worry. I'm a master at it.
> I'll have you a total pro in no time!
> Be over in five x

> **ME:** Amazing thanks so much,
> you are a lifesaver! x

God that was **SO** helpful. Not.

Liv said, 'Right, let's see just what we are dealing with here. Imagine I'm Daniel and I've just walked over to speak to you.'

She lowered her voice into a gruff manly version, which was funny because Daniel sounds nothing like that AT ALL in real life. I thought, *I can deffo do this because it's not Daniel, it's just Liv – easy peasy!*

'Hey, Lottie. What's up?' she began.

Suddenly from nowhere the panic began to rise inside me and the words I wanted to say seemed to float out of reach. My mind went totally blank! **SO** I just opened my mouth and hoped for the best.

'Oh hi . . . um . . . Laniel . . . I mean, Daniel . . . I'm just going to my, um . . . maths lesson. But, um, I'm going to the toilet first. Because I'm desperate for a wee so, um . . . yeh, better go. Don't want to wet myself in school, do I? Ha ha.'

I'm not joking. This was Liv's face . . .

She actually looked scared for me.

The upshot was that Liv felt that I had a little bit more work to do than she had originally thought. Unfortunately, she didn't have all night to help me as she has history coursework due in tomorrow. And, in any case, it would take about three years to sort out my 'problem'. Bit upsetting to hear but probably fair.

She did give me a few quick tips though for dealing with nerves . . .

* Keep calm and speak slowly. (OH WOW – well, if only I had thought of this before! FYI I'm being sarcastic.)

* Imagine the person you are speaking to is naked. (What the?! How on earth would that help? Surely it would make things 1,000,000 times worse.)

* Role-play the conversation with a family member. (As if?! Imagine role-playing asking a boy out with your mum. Or, worse still, your dad. Or, even worse still, your brother! Mega awks.)

So I'm sure with a bit of practice I'm going to be an expert at speaking to boys in no time at all (again, I'm being sarcastic).

SUNDAY 6 MARCH

Decided to try role-playing asking Daniel out with
Professor Squeakington. Fuzzball was too busy sleeping
(again). It went really well actually, so perhaps if I just
imagine Daniel as a hamster we'll finally be able to have
a proper conversation . . .

The translation of his reply for those of you who don't speak Hamster was: 'Yes, that would be absolutely delightful, Lottie! PS you look beautiful today!'

The Professor is such a wee charmer. ☺

MONDAY 7 MARCH

Tried the 'Imagine Daniel as a hamster' technique today but it didn't help at all. In fact, it was blooming terrifying!

In contrast, Molly had a **MUCH** more successful encounter with Theo on the way home . . .

'See ya tomorrow, Molly,' he said as we walked through the school gates.

'If you're lucky!' she replied without missing a beat.

HOW DOES SHE DO THAT?!

'OMG, he totally has the hots for you!' said Jess.

'Do you think?!'

'He specially said goodbye to **YOU!** It must be love,' I said. 'Would you go out with him if he asked you?'

'Ummmm . . . maybe,' she replied in a way that sounded like a big fat **YES**.

TUESDAY 8 MARCH

Back living in the Fort of Shame.

My heart has been shattered into a ~~million billion~~ gazillion pieces.

I'm not sure how I will make it through such great tragedy. Everything feels bleak and pointless.

No one else understands. All I have left in this world are my loyal hamsters and a multipack of KitKat Chunkys (that I bought from Sainsbury's on my way home).

I don't care what threats my parents make (unless they involve the Wi-Fi). I shall never be able to return to school **EVER AGAIN**.

Too dispirited to write more.

5.45 p.m.

I only have one KitKat Chunky left. I feel absolutely terrible. Yes, because of the heartache but mostly from scoffing three KitKat Chunkys in a row. I mean, I like them and all, but three in a row is just madness.

TBH, the heartache could just be indigestion. It's very hard to tell them apart.

6.09 p.m.

Mum is really cross with me. I said I couldn't eat dinner due to the great tragedy of my love life, but she saw the KitKat wrappers on my bedroom floor and didn't believe me. She says that if I can't be trusted to spend my pocket money responsibly, then she will stop giving me it.

She has also confiscated my last KitKat Chunky. I reacted badly to this news, but in retrospect I think it was a wise move.

Suddenly felt hungry again so I crept downstairs and ate the final KitKat.

Mum caught me in the act and now I'm grounded until the weekend. So it turns out that they can take my KitKat **AND** my freedom. Grrrr.

Four KitKat Chunkys is definitely too many. Feel terrible. What an idiot. I think I'm going to die. Should I call 111?

False alarm. I am not dead. Did a really massive chocolatey-flavoured burp and feel MUCH better. It was a nice burp actually, tasted yummy. I quite enjoyed it.

Oh God, that sounds like something Toby would say. I'm so gross – please do not tell anyone I said that!

OK, now I know I have your trust, maybe I'm ready to tell you what happened.

I never got to tell Daniel that I liked him, because at lunch today Amber announced to everyone sitting at our table (me, Jess, Molly, Poppy, Meera and Kylie): 'OMG, have you heard the news about Daniel and Marnie? Marnie told me last week that she has a crush on him, so

I told Luis, who told Ben, who told Theo, who told Daniel, and apparently he has liked her for AGES too!'

I felt a horrible, jealous dread creeping through my body. I wanted to put my fingers in my ears to stop Amber talking.

'So . . . now they are officially boyfriend and girlfriend and it's all thanks to me!' she continued. 'Am I the best at matchmaking in the world or what?'

Everyone started to agree with her, even Molly murmured her approval. It was only Jess who managed to shoot me a sympathetic glance across the table.

I didn't want to listen to any more. I was just about to make an excuse to go to the toilet when Amber turned to me directly and said, 'They make the absolute **CUTEST** couple, don't you think, Lottie?'

'Yeh,' I muttered, about as enthusiastically as I could manage. Then I picked up my bag quickly and made my way out of the canteen. Luckily, it was almost time for next period anyway.

I just feel so cross with myself. All the time I'd been thinking of telling Daniel how I felt, someone else had been doing the same. Now it's too late and it's totally my fault.

I'm also really hurt by Molly's reaction. She didn't seem to care about my feelings at all. When she tried to ask me what was wrong on the way home, I just shrugged it off and said nothing.

7.39 p.m.

WhatsApp conversation with Molly:

MOLLY: Hey Lots, are you mad with me? I get you're upset about Daniel and Marnie but that's not my fault, is it? Xx

ME: It's not your fault but Amber was purposely trying to rub it in my face and you just sat there congratulating her!

MOLLY: She wasn't trying to rub it in your face. She was just telling us the news, that's all. It's not like you and Daniel have ever been a thing and if you'd have wanted to, you could have asked him out.

ME: You know that's not me. I can't just 'ask people out' like that.

MOLLY: Well, it's not Amber's fault that you are too scared to talk to him either!

ME: I know. But it always feels like she's trying to get at me . . . and I would have thought as my best friend you would be on my side!

MOLLY: I'm always on your side. But you need to accept that Amber is my friend too and stop trying to cause problems in the group.

Tears started to swim in my eyes and blur the screen, so I put the phone down. I feel like I've been slapped in the face. How on earth am I meant to respond to that?

Luckily, while I was trying to write a reply she messaged again.

MOLLY: I'm sorry if that was a bit harsh and I'm sorry about Daniel too. I know you really liked him but I just want us all to get along, OK?

ME: OK. I'm sorry too. I don't want us to fall out xx

MOLLY: Never! And listen – Marnie and Daniel will probably be over by the weekend. I hear her longest relationship was 2 3/4 hours!

ME: Well, I have her beat then as mine was a week! The secret is getting together with someone you've never met over half-term 😎

MOLLY: You're so funny, Lottie.
Love ya, nunnite xxx

ME: Love ya too, nunnite xx

So I feel a little bit better about things now. But only a little. Because although Molly can't see it, I know what Amber is trying to do and I don't like it at all.

WEDNESDAY 9 MARCH

7.43 a.m.

Woke up and told Mum I couldn't go to school because I was ill with chocolatoxia (I made it up, but it sounded quite good).

Mum said that if I didn't get ready for school immediately, then she would be changing the Wi-Fi password. Looks like I'm going to school then!

4.24 p.m.

Today was a hard day. Firstly because I only got eight out of thirty on a geography pop quiz about river formations, and secondly because my soul was being tortured by seeing Marnie and Daniel together.

The two things are most probably related **IMO**. I mean, how can I care about river formations when my one true love's heart belongs to another?!

I mean, there is no contest really. Even an oxbow (which is kind of cool TBF) did nothing for me.

I mean, **LOOK AT HIM!!** Seriously how goddam cute is that boy?! OK it may be a bit difficult to tell by my pic but, trust me, he's seriously **HOT**.

Back to Daniel and Marnie . . . I tried my best to avoid them, but unfortunately Marnie's locker is in the same block as mine and at break time they were standing right by it, staring into each other's eyes.

They even have the exact same colour hair

I don't think this will be over by next week . . .

In fact, I think they are already falling in love!

They are probably going to be together forever. They'll probably travel the world and learn seven different languages fluently. They'll probably do loads of charity work and set up a rescue centre for injured wildlife AND they won't even brag about it on Instagram because that's what **GOOD** people are like. They'll probably live in a thatched cottage and grow their own vegetables in the garden **AND** be vegan (not even cheating vegans who 'accidentally' eat slices of four-cheese pizza and Cornettos but REAL ones). They'll probably have twenty-five incredibly well-behaved, sickeningly good-looking children and a really cute puppy called Beau. Maybe they'll save a pig from a farm and call it Babe!!

They'll probably get married and invite the **ENTIRE** school to the wedding and I'll have to go and pretend to be **RIDICULOUSLY HAPPY** for them, because if I don't then everyone will know that I still care about Daniel.

Me pretending not to care (badly)

For goodness' sake – get a grip, Lottie. They've only been together twenty-four hours!

I just don't know how I am going to make it through . . . I feel like I'm in a black-and-white music video about a girl whose heart has been broken and I'm just sitting in my room staring at the walls and looking sad. I wonder if anyone would want to come and film me for a music video, as that could be one positive? I guess they'd also do my hair and make-up as well so that, even though I'm looking sad, at least I'll look sad and gorgeous at the same time. They must use really good waterproof mascara. I wonder what brand it is . . .

6.03 p.m.

Mum's just interrupted my sad sitting-in-my-room music video by asking me to come downstairs and set the dinner table. Honestly, I can't even enjoy feeling sorry for myself any more!

THURSDAY 10 MARCH

4.25 p.m.

I saw D & M holding hands in the playing field at lunchtime. Their relationship is obviously progressing incredibly quickly!

Then, and you won't believe this . . . as I was walking to art class, I saw Dan the Man holding hands with Leggy Lexi! Lexi is the tallest girl in our year by about a foot, so holding hands with her was probably pretty tricky for him . . . but he didn't seem to mind. The quite frankly **HUGE** height difference didn't seem to faze them at all. They just looked ridiculously happy too . . . I mean, I know I should be pleased for them, but would it have killed him to wait a bit longer than two weeks before cruelly replacing me?!

TM

Leggy Lexi

Sigh. Literally **EVERYWHERE** I look **EVERYBODY** seems to be holding hands. Daniel and Marnie . . . DTM and Lexi . . . Well, at least four people anyway . . . There are probably loads of other handholders at school that I just haven't seen yet.

I've never held a boy's hand and I'm twelve and a half now! How is that even fair?!

I'll probably never hold a boy's hand. I will probably end up a crazy cat lady pushing kittens around in a pram!

TBH though that sounds pretty good as kitties are super cute. The only problem is that they may eat my hammies! Eek.

EDIT: Just remembered that hamsters only live around two years so it would be unlikely that they would still be around when I'm ninety-three.

EDIT 2: Unless they broke the world record for world's oldest hammies, which would be AWESOME!!

Not sure if hamsters can actually grow facial hair →

7.24 p.m.

I wonder if D & M have kissed yet? I hope not! I can't bear to think of him kissing another girl.

This is horrible. It's even worse than the time when I was five and left my favourite Elsa dress at Sophia's house. I didn't even like Sophia, but Mum had encouraged me to go on a playdate there – big mistake! Sophia then refused to give the dress back and she said it was hers! It was all so unjust. Eventually our mums got involved and the dress came back, but it had a rip in the skirt and baked-bean juice down the bodice. I didn't like it after that – it just felt tainted and wrong.

Sophia's mum also cooked spaghetti bolognese for tea and it had big chunks of onion in it. I vowed to never go back.

Anyway, my point was it feels just like that but worse!!

FRIDAY 11 MARCH

4.25 p.m.

Jess has just left. She came over after school to stage an intervention because apparently I needed 'a good talking to'! I did feel a bit gutted that Molly didn't come too (I think she thinks that I'm being a bit dramatic) but I'm lucky that Jess gets how I'm feeling as she really helped me make sense of it all.

She told me that if Daniel would rather go out with Marnie than with me, then it's HIS LOSS and that I should not let a boy dictate my happiness!

SHE IS SO RIGHT!!!! I cannot believe I have let myself get so ridiculously upset over him.

I mean, when he eats Wotsits he doesn't lick the cheese powder off properly and I've seen him on numerous occasions with orangey fingernails so he's hardly perfect . . .

Let it be known!
I can do better
than a wotsity-
fingered boy!

* can't really draw stick people with fingers coz it looks weird so2!

Then we put on some Little Mix and danced around my room to 'Power' and 'Shout Out to My Ex' at full volume.

Mum got a bit annoyed because apparently Bella was taking a nap. Honestly, everything in this house revolves around Bella's naps. It's like living in a monastery. Mum could take a bit more interest in her oldest daughter, who has had her heart torn to literal shreds! (OK, maybe not literal, as that would be gross, but you get my point).

I am feeling so much better now. I had a great time – it was a shame that Molly wasn't there, but it was so good to have a proper laugh with Jess again.

AND I won't waste a second longer thinking about Daniel and Marnie and whether they have kissed or not because **I COULDN'T CARE LESS!**

HA!

Do you think they've kissed yet though? I mean, as I say, I obviously couldn't care less . . . I'm simply just a weensy bit curious . . .

THOUGHT OF THE DAY:

I wonder if when he kisses her it tastes of Wotsits?! Unlucky Marnie – that would be gross! I wonder if someone kissed me, would it taste of pickled-onion Monster Munch?! I wonder what crisps are least offensive to eat before kissing someone. I suspect ready salted.

SATURDAY 12 MARCH

3.12 p.m.

Woke up. Felt great. Decided to do something crazy to mark the dawn of the new, independent, much-less-boy-obsessed Lottie!

I went to find Mum and told her I was finally ready to get my ears pierced.

OK, I know it's not exactly that crazy. I've wanted my ears pierced for ages, but the problem is that I'm actually pretty **(VERY)** scared of needles. BUT today I was going to be brave.

Anyway, Mum reluctantly agreed to tear herself away from the hoovering and make me an appointment at a piercing shop in town. Molly already had plans, but Jess said she'd come with me to hold my hand.

My bravery started disappearing the closer and closer we

got to the shop, but I wasn't going to back out – no, not me!

Finally, I sat in the seat and the lady with BIG needles **(ARGH)** began talking me through the process. I started to feel very giddy and sick.

I didn't want to hear about how she was going to do it – I just wanted her to do it quickly!

She put the gun to my ear (why do they call it a gun?!) and I said, 'Actually, no. I've changed my mind!' but everyone just laughed as they thought I was trying to be funny. But I wasn't joking! I was terrified.

Next, I heard a gunshot and everything faded to black.

I thought, *That's it! My time is up* . . . Images of the things I'd never get to do swam through my brain . . . I'll never get to go Christmas shopping in New York, I'll never skydive out of a plane (not that I would anyway – it's madness!), I'll never get my hair balayaged and I'll never know what I look like with pierced ears . . .

I had the feeling of being lifted up and rising, floating along. Then there were muffled voices and then bright halogen lighting – was this heaven?!?

Then a familiar smell . . . salty chips and strawberry milkshake . . . I was OK . . . I was alive . . . I was in McDonald's!

Jess was trying to rouse me by wafting chicken nuggets under my nose.

'Lottie, Lottie . . . are you OK?' said Mum.

'Yes . . . yes . . . I think so. What happened?'

'You fainted in the piercing shop and me and Jess had to carry you through the shopping centre and up the escalator. It was extremely difficult. You were mumbling incoherently about skydiving and getting your hair balayaged.'

'WOW! WELL, THANK GOODNESS I'M ALIVE!'

I exclaimed loudly, much to the amusement of the surrounding tables who looked at me like I was insane.

'Yes, it was a bit touch and go,' Mum said, laughing.

'So how do they look?! Do they look good on me?' I asked Jess as I put my hands up to my ears.

'Ummm . . . well . . .'

'Hang on . . . Why do I only have one earring in?'

I noticed them both exchange nervous glances.

'Look, Lottie, unfortunately they were unable to do your second ear. Apparently it's against shop policy to pierce unconscious people,' said Mum.

'I think it looks pretty cool anyway,' said Jess. 'Certainly original!'

I wasn't convinced, but Mum said we could go back and get the other one done next week if I wanted.

I decided not to worry about it for now, and to focus on the task in hand – getting my strength back by eating an entire sharing box of chicken nuggets. I managed eighteen to be precise, which is a new personal best. I felt so much better after that. Temporarily.

When we got home, Dad was run ragged!

'Why is nobody wearing any clothes?' asked Mum.

'I've barely had time to think, let alone get everybody dressed . . .' replied Dad.

'IT'S PANTS PARTY TIME!' shouted Toby. 'DAD DIDN'T HAVE TIME TO MAKE US LUNCH EITHER, SO I ATE A PACKET OF CHOCOLATE FINGERS AND FIVE BAGS OF CRISPS!'

Mum gave Dad one of her best scary looks.

'Well . . . it's a lot harder than you'd imagine looking after a baby and a . . . a . . . Toby,' he said sheepishly. 'Anyway we have a surprise for you, don't we, Bella?'

He held Bella up and you wouldn't believe it – she looked right into our faces and gave us a huge gummy smile.

Any anger that Mum had left melted away. It was a truly mesmerizing moment, and one that we will all remember forever.

Not least because Dad had put a pair of tights on her head thinking they were a hat . . .

WhatsApp conversation with Molly:

MOLLY: OMG. Are you OK? Saw you being carried through the shopping centre earlier!

ME: I'm fine. I just fainted a little bit when I got my ear pierced, that's all.

MOLLY: Ahhh. Makes sense. We thought you looked drunk!

ME: How would I be drunk?! I'm twelve.

MOLLY: I don't know, that's just what it looked like 😜

ME: THANKS! What were you doing there anyway? I thought you had plans.

MOLLY: Oh, yeh, I did. Just shopping with Amber. Saw you through Zara's window but we were in line for the changing room so we couldn't come out to see you. Do the ears look good??

ME: Er, well one of them does. Yeh.

MOLLY: What do you mean??!

> **ME:** Long story. I'm still feeling slightly woozy so I'll explain later. Hope you had a fun day x

> **MOLLY:** Yeh it was great. See you Mon xx

So, she was 'just shopping with Amber'?!

Just shopping with Amber (MY EVIL NEMESIS) instead of being by my side when **I ALMOST DIED!** Unable to come and see if I was OK in case they **LOST THEIR POSITION IN THE CHANGING-ROOM QUEUE IN ZARA?!**

Hmph. Feeling rather rejected now. Why were they having a secret shopping trip anyway. Where were our invites??

THOUGHT OF THE DAY:
Eating eighteen nuggets is crazy.
Especially when washed down with
a large strawberry milkshake.
Two stars. Do not recommend.

SUNDAY 13 MARCH

My ear has calmed down a bit and looks less red now.

Mum says you have to be very careful caring for piercings so that they don't get infected. I have special solution to apply and I need to twiddle the earring round a few times a day. But also not over-twiddle as that can be bad too. Feels like way too much responsibility.

I really like it though. I keep looking at myself in the mirror – I look so much older and more glamorous. From the left-hand side only obviously.

MONDAY 14 MARCH

I had never spoken to Marnie before today. This is the first thing she has ever said to me:

'Oh gosh, Lottie, are you OK?? Me and Daniel saw you being carried through the shopping centre on Saturday. We thought you looked drunk!'

Did anyone **NOT** see me being carried through the shopping centre on Saturday?

I said, 'I was actually having a near-death experience. Luckily, I'm fine now, but thank you for your concern.'

'Really glad to hear that, Lottie. Daniel was very worried . . . By the way, I think you may have lost an earring.'

Ooooh. Well, that makes it a bit more interesting. Not the earring bit – I knew that. The bit about Wotsit Fingers being worried about me. That was good news!

. . . However, the downside to that is that he was worried about me because (along with half of the school) he thinks I'm an underage drinker! That is bad news!

And there is also another downside . . . Daniel and Marnie have been hanging out together in town and we all know what hanging about together in town leads to, don't we . . . ?

KISSING!!

Well, I don't actually know that TBH. I just imagine it might.

Not that I care any more, obviously.

PS Was told approximately twelve billion times by random people that one of my earrings had fallen out. I didn't have the time or strength to keep repeating the traumatic details of Saturday's events, so I just smiled and thanked them kindly.

TUESDAY 15 MARCH

Word on the street is that Theo is about to ask Molly out!

I thought that was pretty good news but, when I asked Molly about it, she went all funny and awkward. I have my suspicions that it's something to do with Amber because she was acting like Molly's bodyguard and blocking Theo's way whenever he went within five metres of her.

Other news is that I have worked out a way to wear my hair so that I don't keep getting told that my earring is missing. I basically do a right-hand-side low ponytail! Genius. I thought I looked quite cultured and refined . . . until Toby said I looked like, and I quote, 'A stupid bum-bum head!'

Honestly, I worry about that boy's future.

Still . . . it did the job! Nobody bothered me today.

WEDNESDAY 16 MARCH

Rehearsals for *The Little Mermaid* started today. It was cool getting to know some of the other members of the cast.

Prince Eric is being played by a boy called Asher and King Triton is being played by a boy called Josh. They are both in Year Eight, both very good-looking, and now they have star parts in the play it's like they have been catapulted into school superstardom. As you can probably imagine, they are also quite arrogant.

Anyway, we all got to do a run-through of our main songs and Mrs Lane said that I sounded great. She also said that the backing music is going to be pretty loud so not to worry if I do end up going a bit off-key – none of us are professional singers and it's all meant to be good fun. Errr . . . bit of a diss, maybe?

Jess is blummin' phenomenal – seriously. Mrs Lane didn't mention anything about turning the backing music up for her. She could probably do the entire thing a cappella.

I'm happy with my song though – I think it suits my voice pretty well. I'm going to have to keep practising and practising!

Molly, Amber and Poppy didn't have much to do because we won't start incorporating the backing-singer fish into the songs until next week, so they spent the entire time fangirling Josh and Asher. It was quite embarrassing really; Amber was on the floor practically licking their shoes – the girl has absolutely no shame. I'd never act like that around a boy. Ahem.

THURSDAY 17 MARCH

I think Molly is mad with me.

It was raining at lunch so we spent break in our form
room. Me and Jess were chatting about the play and
practising a couple of sections where we have lines
together.

Suddenly Molly huffed and started packing up her things.

'You OK?' I asked.

'No offence, guys, but this is pretty boring for me,' she
said, standing up.

'Sorry . . . we didn't mean to leave you out . . .' said Jess.

'I know, but you could be a bit more understanding . . .
It feels a bit like you are rubbing my face in it.'

I was so shocked I didn't really know what to say.

Over the other side of the room I noticed Amber was suddenly all ears. 'Come over here, Molly. We're compiling a list of the top ten boys in school . . . It's much more fun than boring play stuff.'

Molly grinned, crossed the room and sat down with her and Poppy. Me and Jess tried to carry on rehearsing, but it was really distracting listening to those three giggling.

I feel really hurt now and I don't know how to put it right. Maybe we should have been a bit more sensitive to Molly's feelings, but equally why can't she be happy for me and Jess? It's not our fault we got the parts we did . . . is it?!

7.49 p.m.

I think I have over-twiddled my earring. It started getting all sore and weepy so I took it out and now I can't bear to put it back in again.

It's causing me huge amounts of stress. On top of

everything else I have going on in my life right now . . .

STUFF I HAVE TO WORRY ABOUT . . .

* Manky ear.

* Still need to get other ear pierced
  (possible risk of life).

* ~~Horrible thoughts of Marnie and
  Daniel kissing.~~

* Actually, I crossed that out as I keep
  forgetting that I don't care.

* Molly ditching me (her supposed BFF!) for
  Amber.

* Very loud and irritating siblings (also
  applies to parents).

* Lack of funds due to minuscule levels
  of pocket money.

* My live performance as a singing crustacean.

* My lack of puberty (apart from rubbishy BO!).

* Pressure to learn stuff in boring lessons rather than just daydream.

* Boring homework.

* Boring hair.

* Boring life.

* Just absolutely everything being boring.

FRIDAY 18 MARCH

NEWSFLASH!

Maybe making that whingy list has helped because things have finally started to happen in the, erm . . . boob department!

Sorry if this is TMI, but this morning when I put my bra on I realized it was getting a bit tighter and, sure enough, when I turned sideways on in the mirror there was a definite bump. Or two bumps, to be precise. I mean, still barely there but a definite change.

I ran into Mum on my way to the bathroom.

'Lottie, are you OK? You look like you've seen a ghost,' she said.

'No, nothing like that . . . I think I'm . . . I think . . .'

She gave me a worried look. 'Have you had another bad dream about barking squirrels, scary cacti or getting kissed by boys with beaks?'

'No. I mean, I just woke up and I noticed that my . . . erm . . . I think . . .'

'Because I personally have never heard a squirrel bark, usually they are very timid, and I really don't think most boys have duck –'

'I'm NOT talking about squirrels or ducks, Mother, I'm talking about my boobs!'

'OH, DARLING, WHAT'S WRONG WITH YOUR BOOBS?'

'Mum, shhhh . . . There's nothing wrong with them. They're just finally starting to grow a bit . . . I think.'

'Oh, sweetheart! Are you feeling OK? I remember when I started growing little buds they were quite tender at first.

And, wow, all those hormones kicking in made me quite confused and angry!'

'Muuuuuuum, be quiet! Dad or Toby might hear. Also, you are being mega cringe!'

I mean, 'little buds'?!? I don't know why I tell my mum these things. She always acts as if it's SUCH a big deal. I guess it kinda is, but I don't want the entire street hearing about it, do I?

However, she did say one good thing – in a couple of weeks we could go and get me measured and see if I need a new bra! **WOOHOO!**

7.18 a.m.

A little concerned that the left vague bump is slightly bigger than the right vague bump. Is that normal?!

7.22 a.m.

Actually, I think that the right vague bump is slightly bigger than the left vague bump!

7.25 a.m.

I can't go to school with wonky bumps. What am I going to do?!??!

7.33 a.m.

I've asked Google and apparently different-sized bumps is totally normal – phew!

6.22 p.m.

That was the most excruciatingly awful dinner time in the history of all dinner times.

Picture the scene. We are all sitting round the table eating Mum's infamous cottage pie (infamous for being almost inedible) and we are having polite chit-chat about our days. You know the drill – stuff like:

How was your day? Fine.

How was school? Fine.

How are your friends? Fine.

Did you learn anything interesting? No.

Etc., etc.

Then Toby just goes out of nowhere: 'I learnt something interesting that has happened!'

'Oh yes, Toby, that's great! Let us hear it then,' said Dad.

Then he announced . . .

I looked down at my plate, a deep-red blush creeping up my neck. Dad, meanwhile, started choking on his cottage pie. As I said – the mash is more like cement!

'Oh, well, Toby, that's um . . . that's a bit err . . . that's personal and not really something that Lottie would probably want to discuss at the dinner table,' said Mum, trying to break the awkward silence.

So he goes, 'Why not?'

I mean, who even invented little brothers because I want to have some strong words with them!

'Because it's private, Toby! Now say sorry to your sister,' said Mum.

'OK. Sorry that you are growing boobies, Lottie!'

GREAT. JUST GREAT.

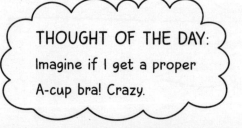

THOUGHT OF THE DAY:
Imagine if I get a proper
A-cup bra! Crazy.

SATURDAY 19 MARCH

Today, the girls came over after school. Me and Jess decided to get the Sylvanians out and make up some daft movie ideas involving them. The best one was called *The Attack of the Killer Hedgehog Family*.

I was laughing so bad in the scene where Mrs Fluffy Bottom was 'accidentally' run over by the school bus that I almost peed my pants. When Jess got Mr and Mrs Prickles to attack Mr Fluffy Bottom with a miniature frying pan, we both absolutely lost it.

'I can't believe you two still play with those things,' said Molly, sighing. She was sitting on my bed, scrolling through her phone.

'We aren't playing with them . . . We're just messing about,' I said defensively.

'You should join in,' said Jess, holding out Petunia Prickles to Molly. But Molly just rolled her eyes without looking up from her screen.

'What are you doing anyway?' I asked, trying to get her involved.

'Oh, just texting Amber . . . She wants to ask Josh and Asher out on a double date.'

So even when she was round my house, hanging with us, she was actually just chatting to Amber. I mean, OK maybe me and Jess were being a bit immature, but at least we were trying to have fun. It's better than just sitting there staring at your phone the whole time, right?!

'I thought you liked Theo?' I said.

'Nah. Not any more.'

'Since when?'

'Well . . . Amber reckons Year Seven boys are **WAY** too young for us.'

'Oh right.'

I looked between my two best friends and suddenly realized how different they are. I have Jess, who is silly, goofy and still into Sylvanian Families, and I have Molly, who is cool, confident and planning on going on an **ACTUAL** date with an **ACTUAL** Year Eight boy.

And then there is me – stuck somewhere in the middle, trying to bridge the gap. On days like today the gap feels wider than ever and maybe, before long, it will be impossible for us all to keep swimming in the same direction.

'Come on, Lottie,' said Jess. 'Finley Fluffy Bottom is dangerously close to getting his ears removed with a saw!'

I smiled and picked up Finley Fluffy Bottom, pretending to make him run and hide from the Killer Hedgehogs in the treehouse. But what Molly had said put a real dampener on it, and it just didn't feel the same any more.

SUNDAY 20 MARCH

The worst news.

My ear is healing over already.

MONDAY 21 MARCH

More rehearsals today.

I think my singing went OK, but Mrs Lane said, 'It does sound good, Lottie, but I'm not getting many crab-like vibes from you. Could we go from the top, and this time try to give me a bit more crabby ooompf?'

Crabby ooompf?!

What on earth was she talking about??

I did the whole thing again but just kind of squatted down a bit to make myself a bit wider, put my arms out to the side and did pincer movements with my hands. It made the singing harder and, to be honest with you, I felt I looked ridiculous, but Mrs Lane said, 'Excellent work, Lottie – that's a huge improvement!'

Bonkers.

TUESDAY 22 MARCH

Crikey. Well, it's all go go go in the puberty arena! If puberty was an arena, which it, er . . . isn't.

Molly got her period.

It was in maths, our last lesson of the day, and I was stuck trying to work out a particularly tricky equation . . .

Question 4: 2x + 21 = 4x + 5

What is x?

Answer:

Who even cares?
Why would I ever
need to Know this?!

Molly was sitting a few desks down from me and when she put her hand up I assumed she was going to ask for some help.

But instead she just said, 'Sorry, sir, but I don't feel well.'

She looked pretty pale, to be honest.

Mr Peters looked up and agreed that she did look a bit peaky. Then he asked for a volunteer to accompany Molly to the school nurse.

'OH! ME, ME, ME!' said Amber, practically leaping out of her chair like an annoying jack-in-the-box.

They went off together and the lesson dragged on and on and on. I looked at the clock and there were only five minutes left of school and they still hadn't come back. Me and Jess were getting pretty worried that Molly must be really sick or something, so after maths had **FINALLY** finished we went to investigate.

We found Molly and Amber by the nurse's office.

Molly still looked quite pale, but she was trying to smile. When Amber saw us coming over, she gave Molly a big dramatic hug and as soon as we were in earshot she said, 'Don't thank me – that's what friends are for!'

'What's going on? Are you OK?' I asked.

'Yes, I'm fine,' Molly said quietly, beckoning us both to lean in. 'I just got IT, that's all.'

'IT?!' I said.

'My period,' she whispered.

'OH MY GOD!' I shrieked.

'Oh, Lottie, calm down,' said Amber in a rather patronizing tone. 'I don't think she wants to announce it to the **ENTIRE** school.'

'Sorry,' I replied, feeling a bit stupid.

After we'd walked Jess home, Molly asked if I'd like to

come to hers for tea. I think she was kind of nervous to tell her mum, Ellie, about getting her period and she thought it might be better to have me there too. Both our mums are pretty similar in that respect, as in they tend to get overexcited and start going on about the dreaded 'journey into womanhood'!

Molly needn't have worried though – she just blurted it out as soon as we walked through the door and her mum was totally great. She gave her a big hug too, and then they disappeared upstairs for a chat while I watched a bit of TV.

When they came back down, we went to sit at the kitchen table and Ellie made us both hot chocolates.

'I'm so glad you were there with her when it happened, Lottie,' Ellie said.

'Um, I . . .'

'It wasn't Lottie who helped me actually, Mum. It was a new friend called Amber.'

'Oh well, I'm so glad you've made such a lovely new friend already, Mol. It sounds like Amber took good care of you.'

'Yes, she really did.'

I smiled at them both, but inside I felt sad that I hadn't been there to help Molly when she really needed me. Worse still, the person who had been there was her new BFF, Amber.

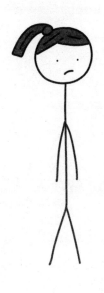

WEDNESDAY 23 MARCH

Amber has invited us all to a roller disco on Saturday
night. Well, to be honest she invited Molly, who then
invited me, who then invited Jess.

I tried to say no because roller skating is really not my
thing, but Molly says that a Girls' Night Out is just what
I need to distract me from the whole Marnie and Daniel
situation. (Why do people keep saying that? I mean, they
could go and get engaged tomorrow and I wouldn't even
bat an eyelid.) I'm desperate to get our friendship back
on track though, so I said yes. I can't help but feel pretty
uneasy about it because . . .

1. I'm not very good at roller skating.

2. When I say 'not very good', I mean **AWFUL**.

3. Molly is a brilliant skater and I bet Amber
   will be too.

4. As usual, Amber will probably find loads of
   ways to put me down and make me feel bad.

5. Jess says she is also a terrible skater, but she can't come be my wing woman as she's visiting her Auntie Irie. **#sadtimes**

6. As usual, I have **NOTHING** to wear.

7. Promised my hamsters we'd have a pamper party on Saturday night and I really don't like to let them down at short notice.

Now, remember guys— the cucumber is for your eyes and NOT for eating!

oops.

THURSDAY 24 MARCH

4.25 p.m.

Oh God, I have a spot. Hang on, let me correct that – a spot has me. It's absolutely huge!

My skin was fine yesterday and then as soon as it gets a sniff of a night out it's all like, **HA HA HA** – here's a humongous zit to ruin all your plans! How is that even fair?

Why can I never seem to catch a break?

6.28 p.m.

Just typed 'how to get rid of a spot' into Google and it came back with 414,000,000 results!

I mean, how is that helpful?! I don't have time to visit millions of websites – can't everyone just agree on the number-one best way to get rid of a spot?! So far, I have read that I should . . .

- ★ Put toothpaste on it.

- ★ Put tea-tree oil on it.

- ★ Put honey on it.

- ★ Put lemon juice on it.

- ★ Put ice on it.

- ★ Put a warm flannel on it.

- ★ Wash my face more often.

- ★ Stop washing my face so often.

- ★ Squeeze it gently.

- ★ Don't even think about squeezing it.

      ★ Slather my entire face in Marmite and
          walk round my bedroom backwards three
          times while clucking like a chicken.

I mean, I might have made up that last one, but I
wouldn't be surprised if that was an actual suggestion
somewhere.

6.33 p.m.

I've decided that the spot needs a name so I've named
her Barbara.

Barbara the volcano is threatening to erupt and cover
everyone in a ten-mile radius in disgusting pus.

Beware Mount Barbara!

6.37 p.m.

Most reputable sources suggest squeezing spots is not
a good idea so I definitely won't be squeezing Mount
Barbara.

She does look super squeezable though . . .

BUT, as I said, I'm definitely not going to do that.

No way.

Nuh-uh.

Not me.

My hands are firmly under my bottom.

6.46 p.m.

OOPS – some squeezing may have occurred! It wasn't
really my fault – my fingers developed a mind of
their own.

The bad news is that Mount Barbara has now taken over
my entire face. I mean, like literally you can hardly see my
face. Well, I guess not literally, but almost.

It's a shame you can't see her in real life so you can understand the **TRUE HORROR**. Oh, hang on, I'll draw you a picture.

Mount Barbara!

close up

Mwah ha ha ha!

SEE. I told you she was bad!

8.14 p.m.

It has just dawned on me that Mount Barbara is going to have to accompany me to school tomorrow.

URGH. Maybe I can wear a paper bag over my head for the day?

Cut out eye holes and smiley mouth

cut off corner for pony tail

No one will notice any difference!!

Smothered entire face in honey. And toothpaste. And a bit of Marmite, because what harm can it do? I'm now going to have to go to sleep on my back and not move a muscle.

I might have done a bit of backwards chicken walking too, but shhhhhh – don't tell anyone.

FRIDAY 25 MARCH

Bit of an emergency this morning.

DO NOT . . . I repeat, **DO NOT** . . . apply a mixture of honey, toothpaste and Marmite to your face before going to bed.

I woke up glued to the pillow. Took me ages to free myself. The eyebrows were particularly painful.

The worst part of it was that I made all that effort and Mount Barbara is still there. In fact, I think she seems even more angry. Maybe she didn't like being covered in honey, toothpaste and Marmite either.

There is **NO WAY** I'm going to school looking like this. My hair absolutely stinks.

7.47 a.m.

Told Mum I was feeling dreadful and that I couldn't go to school. She asked me what was wrong and for maximum sympathy I decided to up the stakes.

'I'm afraid I think I've got the bubonic plague.'

She said, 'Oh well, that's convenient because the death cart is coming round this afternoon, so we'll just chuck you right on that if you aren't going to school.'

'I'm being serious, Mum. I can't go to school – have you seen my face?!'

'Yes, I see it every day. It's like a beautiful sunbeam.'

'What, even when it's been taken over by a huge volcanic eruption?'

'Lottie, I can barely even see this so-called huge volcanic eruption and you are certainly not the first tweenager in the world to get a spot. Now stop being ridiculous and get dressed!'

Sigh. Looks like me and Mount Barbara are off to school for show and tell.

(4.27 p.m.)

First thing Amber said to me was: **'OH MY GOD, Lottie!** You poor thing. It must be terrible having bad skin. Luckily, I've been blessed with good family genes in that area.'

Oh, go and do one, Amber!

Spent most of the day sitting with my head in my hands and trying to hide Mount Barbara from view.

After school I asked Mum to drive me into town to buy

some spot cream. Dad was still at work and she wasn't particularly keen to drag Bella and Toby into town at teatime, but I don't think she fully understood the gravity of the situation!

OK, it wasn't the easiest trip . . . Bella screamed all the way there and back, which was pretty irritating, and Toby got reprimanded by the security guard in Boots for doing knee slides down the aisles. We were so embarrassed that me and Mum decided to disown him!

Luckily, it was worth the pain, because I found a spot cream that promises clearer skin in four hours. Just put a blob on Mount Barbs. Fingers crossed it works!

8.27 p.m.

It didn't work! How do they get away with advertising this sort of stuff if it's not true?!

It's like the seventy-two-hour deodorant I bought that promised I would only need to shower every three days. Absolute lies.

SATURDAY 26 MARCH

Mount Barbara update: still here. Looks worse.

Mum said that my restrictive diet of margherita
pizza, nuggets, Pot Noodles, Monster Munch and KitKat
Chunkys is probably not helping. She may have a point.
Did some research and apparently 'protein-rich' foods
are good for your skin. These include:

* Chicken

* Fish

* Kidney beans

* Low-fat natural yoghurt

* Eggs

* Chia seeds

So, being the uber-helpful daughter that I am, I told

Mum and Dad to go and sit down while I made everyone lunch – and they were really touched!

Went through the cupboards and found *most* of the stuff, with a few substitutions.

First, I put some chicken dippers into a large pan and turned on the hob. It did say to oven cook them but I was sure this would work too. Then I tipped in a can of tuna – so that was the fish part covered. (Maybe I should have drained the brine first but hey ho.) We didn't have any kidney beans so I used baked beans, which are much nicer anyway. Couldn't find any 'natural yoghurt', whatever that is, but we had a couple of Müller Corners (with chocolate cornflakes – yum!) and five Frubes so I emptied those in too. Then I gave it all a good stir.

Mum shouted, 'Um, Lottie . . . just wondering what you are making as it smells . . . errrrr . . . interesting?'

'Oh, don't worry, Mum – it's a surprise. It will be delicious, I promise!'

Hmmm, I thought. *What's next? . . . Aha! Eggs.*

I didn't know whether the eggs should be fried, boiled or poached so I just cracked them straight in the mix. The final ingredient was chia seeds but we didn't seem to have any of those either. The only things that came close were sunflower seeds, which we give to the hammies, and a bag of dry roasted peanuts. I couldn't decide which would work best so I added both.

LOVELY STUFF!

I cooked it for another few minutes and then I spooned it all on to plates and called for everyone to come and get it. It was the first time I'd prepared a proper home-cooked meal for the family so I was feeling dead proud of myself.

'Oh . . . um . . . this looks . . . nice?' said Dad.

'What . . . erm . . . is it?' said Mum.

'It's called Barbara's Demise!'

And would you believe it? They were dead rude about my efforts! Dad and Mum took the tiniest bites I've ever seen and then made faces like they were in physical pain. I mean, they could at least have pretended to like it.

Then I tried a mouthful!

OMG, HEAVE!

Unfortunately, it seems that the chicken dippers were still frozen solid because apparently they needed cooking for longer than five minutes. Oops.

I don't think that was the only problem TBH. Tuna, Frubes and baked beans is certainly an acquired taste.

Toby ate the most out of all of us. He said he quite liked the frozen chicken dippers covered in chocolatey yoghurt flakes.

It's a bit like a magnum but with chicken inside instead of ice cream!

He's a strange, strange child.

The Queens of Seven Green WhatsApp group:

AMBER: Hey guys, Molly's already over at my house so we'll meet you outside the leisure centre at 6.30 OK? Looking forward to skating later X

ME: Sure OK. What are you guys wearing?

MOLLY: Not sure yet, nothing special X

AMBER: Yeh, just going dead casual.

POPPY: Cool. Joggers it is then! See you there X

JESS: Wish I was coming – have fun, everyone! xx

So Molly and Amber are both together at Amber's house. It's hard not to feel upset but I can't help it. How come the two of them keep getting together without the rest of us? And it seems Poppy isn't with them either.

5.55 p.m.

You won't believe my luck!

Sometimes Mum leaves Bella with her clothes off for ten minutes or so to give her skin a chance to breathe. It's called Naked Time. I said I hoped Mum didn't do Naked Time when I was younger and she said I was mostly fully naked until the age of four. This is not something I wanted to know – also why didn't she insist I put clothes on, for goodness' sake??

Anyway . . . during today's Naked Time, Bella decided she needed a poo. Have you ever seen newborn-baby poo? It looks like mustard and it's all sloppy, but the worst thing is that Bella can shoot it out of her bottom at sixty miles per hour.

So there I was all ready to go out in my most presentable joggers and tee, gently tickling her cute lil' tum to make her smile and BAM . . .

I was absolutely fuming and I may have taken it out on Mum . . .

'Bella's just pooed all over my clothes and now I've got absolutely nothing clean to wear because no one ever seems to do any laundry any more!'

She absolutely lost it. 'For goodness' sake, Lottie, the world does not revolve around you! Can't you see how hard I'm working, trying to keep the house clean and you

lot fed? Would it kill you to do your own washing
for once?!'

Then I made a big mistake – I did a huge dramatic sigh.

Mum looked like she was going to cry and dashed out
of the lounge. I think I'd have preferred it if she'd kept
shouting at me.

I didn't have time to apologize as I was already running
late. I just went up to my room and grabbed the least
scuzzy things I could find in my laundry bin. I dreaded to
think what Amber would say, but at least it was only us
girls.

8.47 p.m.

Just got home. It was awful. Everything that could go
wrong did go wrong.

Dad dropped me off outside the King Alfred leisure
centre and Molly and Amber were already waiting there.
As I walked up to them, my heart dropped. They weren't
'dead casual' as Amber had said – instead they looked

effortlessly cool in flared jeans and crop tops. I was used to Amber looking incredible 24/7 but I'd never seen Molly look so beautiful before. It was almost like looking at a different person. Her hair was curled in waves like you see on models in magazines, and her make-up was flawless. She had peach lipstick on that looked gorgeous against her pale skin, and perfect flicked eyeliner.

I looked down at my crinkled T-shirt (complete with suspect stain – sweet 'n' sour sauce maybe?!) and faded joggers and my heart sank. Especially when I remembered Mount Barbara (that no amount of concealer would cover).

Them looking like a fashion advert

me looking like I slept in a bin

At least I wasn't the only one though. When Poppy turned up, it was clear she hadn't got the memo either.

We must have looked upset as Molly turned to Amber and said, 'I thought you'd messaged them to say that we'd decided to ditch the joggers idea.'

Amber put on a 'poor me' face and took her phone out of her bag. 'Oh no!' she said, showing it to Molly. 'I did. Look, there's the message. I typed it out, but I must have got distracted and not hit send.'

'I'm sorry, guys,' Molly said. 'It was a last-minute thing. Amber said she'd do my hair and make-up and then it all just looked a bit silly with tracksuit bottoms . . . so I borrowed some jeans . . . and a top . . .'

'Oh, me toooooooo,' said Amber. 'Anyway, you look . . . um . . . fab. And it doesn't matter what we're wearing as we're just here to have a laugh, right?'

I muttered, 'Yeh,' but inside I felt so cross with them. I didn't look 'fab'; I looked awful. It looked like two trendy teenagers were taking their nine-year-old sisters out with them.

As predicted, I was the worst roller skater at the **ENTIRE** roller disco. So, while the others were skating round the hall looking like total pros, I was stuck going super slow round the edges and flailing my arms around trying not to fall over.

Think it can't get any worse? **WRONG.**

Josh and Asher arrived and suddenly Molly and Amber lost their minds and went into MEGA flirt mode. Apparently it was 'a total coincidence' that they were there, although I strongly suspect that Amber had planned this all along. So much for our 'Girls' Night Out', hey?

It wasn't long before Asher and Amber and Molly and Josh were skating around holding hands and I was left feeling like a right lemon. Why had they dragged me along on this weird double date? Was it just to rub my face in it?

My feet were absolutely killing so I went for a sit-down. Not that Molly even noticed. I must have sat there on my own for about fifteen minutes. Eventually (and probably because they felt sorry for me) Molly and Josh came over and grabbed me by the hand and said I should skate with them – which in a way made me feel even more like a loser.

But they started going way too fast for my skill level, so I ended up losing my balance, flying across the room and falling badly on to my bottom in front of everyone. The worst part was that it absolutely killed, but I really didn't want them to see me cry, so I had to pretend I was fine and that I found it really funny.

Spotty Lottie fell badly on her botty!

I'd had enough by this point, so I was about to go and call Dad and get him to come pick me up early. But then, like a knight in shining armour, Jess appeared!

'What are you doing here?' I said.

'We got back from Auntie Irie's early, so I thought I'd come and surprise you.' She helped me to my feet and I blinked the tears from my eyes. Then she asked, 'Why is Poppy sitting on her own over there?'

I'd completely forgotten about Poppy . . . I felt terrible thinking that she'd been sitting in a dark corner just like me. 'I guess maybe she was ditched too?'

We skated (badly) over to Poppy, and Jess grinned at her and grabbed her hand. 'Come on! If this is a roller disco, then why aren't we dancing?!'

We spent the rest of the night doing really awful (but hilarious) skating/dancing – Jess didn't even seem to care how terrible she was. When they started playing Justin Bieber, we went absolutely crazy!

Molly and Amber and the boys largely just sat at the
edge of the room chatting; sometimes they'd look in our
direction and laugh. Maybe they were talking about how
silly we were being, but at least we were having fun!
Then, when it was time to go, and we were waiting for
Ellie to come and collect us, all Molly and Amber could
talk about was how hot and dreamy Asher and Josh were.
It was like me, Jess and Poppy were invisible.

I went straight up to my room when I got in. Mum and Dad were busy with Toby and Bella – and no one has come in to ask how my night was. I feel like I'm being left behind. I feel like I'm losing my best friend and there doesn't seem to be anything I can do to stop it.

SUNDAY 27 MARCH

(8.32 a.m.)

Woke up to Toby banging on my door like the house was on fire.

'Lottie, wake up! Mum's fuming!'

'What is it? . . . What's wrong?!'

He grabbed me by the shoulders and started to shake me. 'It's Mother's Day!'

OH. MY. GOD.

Yes, dear reader, we had completely forgotten.

'She thought we'd forgotten –'

'We had forgotten . . .'

'Yes, but I didn't want her to know that we'd forgotten . . .

so I told her I was waiting for you to get out of bed because we had a **REALLY GREAT** joint present. She's taken Bella out for a walk and Dad's still asleep – we have to get her something ASAP or she'll be livid!'

'OK, don't panic, little bro. We'll come up with a plan. Let's look around the house – there has to be something giftable here.'

'OK, big sis, let's do it.'

'And, Toby . . .'

'Yeh?'

'You can stop shaking me now.'

'OK.'

8.55 a.m.

We have reconvened with our prospective gifts. This is what we have:

* Almost-full can of deodorant (used approx. three to five sprays)

* Ball of Blu-Tack

* Inflatable brachiosaurus

* New washing-up sponge

* Tin of pineapple chunks

* A bottle of her own wine

* Half a packet of Polos

* Five Nerf gun bullets

* A rock (Toby's idea obvs – apparently it's a good one – why?!)

* ~~KitKat Chunky~~ (probably the best option until I accidentally ate it – OOPS!)

Hmm . . . not feeling very confident that any of our gift ideas will do the job, to be honest . . . Toby says he has another idea though, so hold tight!

9.12 a.m.

OK, so Toby's idea was based on something they did at school for World Book Day where they had to make a potato look like their favourite character from a book. He thought we should do one for Mum because it would show we made a proper effort. For want of a better idea, I agreed. We used yellow wool for the hair, matches for the arms and legs, googly eyes, and completed the look with a lovely shade of cherry-red lipstick. This is the result . . .

POTATO MUMMY!

Hope she likes it!

I don't think Mum did like it. She ended up in tears when she saw the potato version of herself. Not sure if they were tears of happiness or tears of despair?

I blame Toby. At the last minute he decided it would be fun (?!) to light Potato Mummy's arms and legs!

The matches then ended up setting the wool hair on fire, so Dad had to grab Potato Mummy and throw her in the sink. And that was the end of that.

WhatsApp conversation with Molly:

MOLLY: U OK? I'm so sorry about the mix-up with the outfits yesterday. Amber really did think she'd texted you the change of plan.

ME: Yeh, I'm OK. I guess I was a bit gutted because you ended up spending all your time with the boys.

MOLLY: We didn't know they were going to be there, Lottie. That wasn't our fault and I tried to get you to skate with us. You could have made a bit of an effort too.

ME: You left me on my own for ages!

MOLLY: We weren't supposed to be babysitting you! Sometimes it feels that just because things didn't work out with you and Daniel that you don't want anyone else to have a boyfriend either.

ME: That's not true. I just don't believe that the boys just 'turned up'. Amber obviously planned the entire thing!

MOLLY: That's ridiculous! You've got to stop being so jealous of Amber.

ME: I'm not jealous. It's just it was supposed to be a girls' night . . .

MOLLY: Well, no offence but dancing to Justin Bieber is not really our thing.

ME: You used to love JB!

MOLLY: Yeh, I used to. But we're in high school now and things are different.

My cheeks flushed and I couldn't stop the tears from falling. We'd never argued like this before. Everything that I'd worried about was coming true.

Tried to chat to Mum about Molly, but she said she didn't have time for my 'tweenage dramas' today. I said that I thought that on Mother's Day she'd want to spend more quality time with her wonderful children. She said she was more interested in spending quality time **ALONE** in a dark room.

All the effort we went to with her handmade gift, and this is the thanks we get . . . How ungrateful.

THOUGHT OF THE DAY:
If mums get a Mother's Day and dads get a Father's Day, then why don't children get a Children's Day?! Seems grossly unfair to me. ☹

TUESDAY 29 MARCH

The last couple of days have been hard. Dad seems tired, Mum's still being moody about #flamingpotatomummygate, Toby's having nightmares that Potato Mummy is going to come back and burn the house down, and although Molly and I have basically pretended that our WhatsApp fight didn't happen . . . there's an obvious divide in the group now.

Molly and Amber on one side and me and Jess on the other. Poppy seems to be stuck somewhere in the middle – perhaps she feels like she's losing her best friend too?

The great divide

I've tried to casually chat to Molly about it a couple of times, but any time I hint that Amber is trying to drive a wedge between us she just says something like, 'She's actually a really great friend. If you took the time to get to know her properly, you'd get it. Plus, it's great to have someone to talk to who actually understands what I'm going through.'

Ouch.

WEDNESDAY 30 MARCH

We were rehearsing the wedding scene today where Ariel marries Prince Eric. Or, if you like, Jess marries Asher! As you can imagine, Amber was absolutely seething with jealousy from the wings, wishing that it was her and Asher instead.

Jess looked strangely uncomfortable though.

'Is everything OK, Jess?' asked Mrs Lane.

'To be honest, miss, I don't like this scene because I don't understand why Ariel is marrying a guy she's only just met – I mean, would that really happen? I certainly wouldn't be marrying someone just because they were a rich, handsome prince. What if he turned out to be super annoying?'

'That's a really good point, Jess, so what would you suggest?'

'Well, I was thinking that maybe we could end the play with them going out for a date or something?'

'I love that idea! Does anyone have any ideas of where we could set the scene for their first date?'

'Yes, I do, miss!' I said. 'The Sea Life Centre!'

I was joking really, but Mrs Lane decided it would make the perfect setting for the big finale.

THURSDAY 31 MARCH

SO relieved. I decided to make the first move and I'm so glad I did.

> **ME:** Hey you, I hate feeling like things are weird between us! Miss you x

> **MOLLY:** So glad you messaged – me too! How about a sleepover at mine on Sat night? It will be just like old times! xx

> **ME:** Yes to the sleepover. I'd love that. Can't wait 😉 x

HUGE relief!

I ran downstairs to tell my parents the plan. I found them drinking coffee in the kitchen. I guess they had had another rough night with the Sleep Thief AKA Bella.

'Molly's invited me for a sleepover on Saturday!' I announced.

Dad looked kind of disappointed. 'Oh . . . it's just that me and Mum were thinking that maybe we could do something together this weekend . . . Bowling maybe?'

'Or a movie night here,' said Mum.

'No offence, guys, but I think I'd rather see my best friend.'

'OK . . . It's just we've all been a bit distracted lately and I thought that maybe some quality family time together would be nice?'

'Errr . . . yeh . . . sure, another time maybe.'

I didn't want to be mean but right now I needed more 'quality family time' like I needed a hole in the head.

FRIDAY 1 APRIL

I absolutely **LOVE** April Fool's Day. That's a lie. I hate it.

Annoyingly it's my little brother's favourite day of the year, and every year his pranks get more and more ridiculous. This year's included:

* Putting googly eyes on pretty much everything in the house

* Putting a fake poo on the loo seat

* Adding green food colouring to the milk

* Putting plastic cockroaches in the cornflakes

* Stuffing the end of my shoes with toilet paper

* AND setting the contents of my pencil case in jelly!

I didn't mind the last one so much as he used strawberry flavour, which is my favourite, so I just ate the pens, rulers and rubbers out of it. It was yummy but it made me v late for school.

When I finally walked into my tutor room, Mr Peters was halfway through the register and everyone looked up at me and burst out laughing. I had no idea what was wrong so when I got to my desk I took my pocket mirror out of my bag to check . . . The little menace had used joke toothpaste and my teeth looked all black and rotten!

SATURDAY 2 APRIL

5.33 p.m.

SO EXCITED ABOUT TONIGHT!

The best thing about sleepovers at Molly's is that I'm almost part of the family, so it just feels a bit like my home too (except all her family members are less annoying). I don't need to be embarrassed about packing all my best loserville stuff because I can totally be myself around there. This is what I'm taking . . .

- 'Just rolled out of bed' Sushi PJs ✓
- Flying squirrel onesie ✓
- unicorn slippers ✓
- Bunny rabbit sleeping bag ✓
- Koala eye mask ✓
- multipack pickled onion monster munch ✓
- LoADS of Kitkat Chunkys ✓
- Teddy One Eye ✓

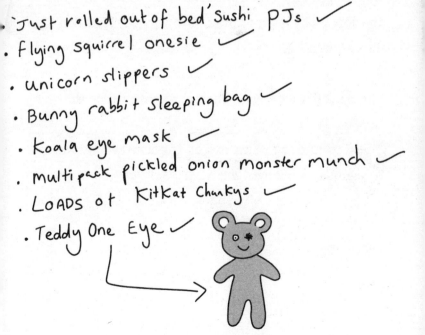

Dad's dropping me round at six so I've already put my PJs, onesie and slippers on – that way I don't have to waste any time getting changed when I'm there.

Oh and FYI Teddy One Eye is my most treasured cuddly. I've had him since the day I was born!

(11.15 p.m.)

Sigh. I'm home again. It didn't go to plan. At all.

Dad dropped me off and as soon as I'd walked through the door Molly grabbed me and whispered, 'Now don't get cross, Lottie . . .'

I immediately didn't like where this conversation was going.

'Amber WhatsApped me earlier. She asked what I was doing today. I told her I was having a sleepover with you and she said, "Oh that's nice," but she sounded really down . . .'

I didn't like it one bit.

'Then she started crying . . . Apparently her parents were at a wedding, and she'd be alone **ALL** day . . .'

I could see exactly how this was going to end.

'I felt SO bad for her that I thought maybe I could ask her to join us . . .'

I'm thinking, *Please say she said no!*

'. . . and she said she'd absolutely love to!'

Fabulous.

'Now I know that you two haven't always seen eye to eye so I started thinking . . . maybe this would be a great opportunity for you to put all that behind you. I've already spoken to Amber about it and I know she'd love it if you guys could make a fresh start. Honestly, give her a chance – she is so sweet!'

I said, **'SHE'S ABOUT AS SWEET AS A CHAINSAW!'**

Except I didn't say that, because I'm not that rude . . . and also it was offensive to chainsaws.

I just said, 'OK, cool.'

'Brilliant. I'm so glad you said that because she's already here!'

Oh. So she wasn't really asking my permission, was she?

We went up to Molly's bedroom and Amber appeared, looking all wide-eyed and innocent. 'Hi, Lottie! I really hope you don't mind me gatecrashing your sleepover.'

'No, not at all,' I said through gritted teeth.

'Oh wow . . . I love your onesie. I used to have one like that when I was six.'

That was when I suddenly became very aware that they were wearing almost-identical cami tops and shorts and I was dressed as a giant flying squirrel.

(Really pleased with my onesie drawing above,
so that's one good thing about tonight!)

I looked at Molly. 'Why aren't you wearing your flying
squirrel onesie?' We'd bought matching versions three
years ago and have worn them at every sleepover since.

'Oh . . . I . . . err . . . must have left it behind in Oz, I guess,'
she said sheepishly.

'You left it behind?!'

'I was growing out of it, Lottie. Anyway, Amber bought me this little PJ set to thank me for hosting. Isn't it, cute?'

'Yeh, you look great. Maybe it's time to retire the flying squirrels anyway. I guess we are getting a bit old for them.'

'Exactly! I mean . . . they do look *quite* babyish . . .'

I started to pull the onesie down. I thought to myself . . . *Don't let it bother you.* And I tried really hard, I promise I did, but from then on the evening just got worse and worse.

You see, Amber has a way of taking over conversations and making sure things always go her way. It began to feel really difficult for me to join in . . .

★ First, she launched into an incredibly detailed review on the different types of sanitary protection on the market and dealing with period pain. Every time I tried to offer some advice, she'd say something like, 'Lottie, no offence, but I don't think you can really understand until it happens to you.'

* When it was time to order pizza, she said she didn't like pepperoni! **WHAT?!** Me and Molly **ALWAYS** get pepperoni pizza. Amber wouldn't even get a half and half in case any of the pepperoni juice leaked on to her side! So I ended up getting a small pizza and Molly agreed to share a large one with her. I mean, I wouldn't normally mind having my own pizza, but it just made me feel like I was at a lonely pizza party for one.

* Also . . . her favourite toppings were ham, pineapple and mushroom. I mean, I don't mind the ham, but people who like putting fruit on a pizza need to have a word with themselves and as for mushrooms?! They are the work of the devil.

* Every movie I suggested she said she had already seen or 'looked really lame' so then we ended up watching *Twilight* because it's her absolute favourite.

* After the movie had finished, they talked about how fun it would be if Molly got together with Asher and Amber got together with Josh and how they could all go out on a double date together.

Like *HELLO . . . I'm still here . . . What about me?* When she did finally remember me, she said, 'Ahhh, we'd invite you too, Lottie, if you had someone who liked you . . .' and then put on a really fake sad face.

★ She said pickled-onion Monster Munch were 'so gross' because they made your breath stink. Then Molly agreed with her and didn't eat **ANY** either!

★ Here is the absolute worst bit. Amber laughed at Teddy One Eye! How could she? She said, 'I can't believe you still carry that mangy, falling-to-pieces old thing around with you, Lottie!' Worse still, Molly didn't stick up for him either and she's known him almost as long as me. Poor Teddy One Eye was devastated!

It was the final insult! I couldn't listen to any more. So I rolled up my sleeping bag and started packing all my things back into my bag. You wouldn't believe this, but they barely even noticed . . . so I started packing them really **LOUDLY** and **ANGRILY**.

After about a million years, Molly turns round and goes, 'What are you doing, Lottie?'

'I'm going home.'

'Why? What's wrong?!'

'Nothing. I'm fine. I just want to . . . go.'

'You aren't fine. You're obviously cross . . . Have we upset you?'

I tried to keep the anger in, but I couldn't help it. 'You're totally ignoring me. This was meant to be our night and instead it's just turned into the Molly and Amber Show!'

'What? Don't be ridiculous. How are we ignoring you?'

'You keep talking about stuff I can't get involved in. It's like I'm invisible!'

Amber sighed. 'Look, Lottie, it's hardly our fault that you don't have a boyfriend and it's hardly our fault that you don't have your period yet, is it?'

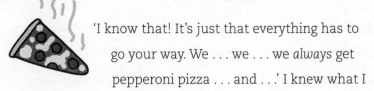

'I know that! It's just that everything has to go your way. We . . . we . . . we *always* get pepperoni pizza . . . and . . .' I knew what I was trying to say but I just couldn't seem to get the right words to come out.

'It's just pizza, Lottie! It's no big deal,' said Molly.

Amber laughed. 'This is SO silly. Molly is allowed to have other friends, you know. Maybe you just need to grow up a bit and accept that . . . I mean, look –' she gestured at my slippers and pyjamas – 'this is all very *primary school*, isn't it?'

I felt the tears spring up in my eyes. I didn't want them to have the satisfaction of seeing me cry so I grabbed the last of my stuff and ran out of the room. When I got downstairs, I told Ellie I wasn't feeling well and asked her to call Dad to come and pick me up. Even though it was 11 p.m., he wasn't cross and said I should always call him or Mum if I'm ever feeling uncomfortable anywhere.

Now I'm back home and safely snuggled up with Teddy One Eye. He didn't deserve this kind of treatment either.

I just feel so let down. It was like Amber and Molly were in some sort of secret club and I wasn't allowed to be a member. Instead of the evening being like old times, I began to feel like the spare part who was gatecrashing the party. How did that happen?

There was a small bit of good news though. When I was unpacking, I realized I still had four bags of Monster Munch left, so me and Teddy One Eye scoffed the rest of them in bed.

you aren't a mangy old thing you are just well loved.

THOUGHT OF THE DAY:
I wonder if I will be the last girl
in the entire Year Seven to get
her period? Probably.

SUNDAY 3 APRIL

Despite the late night last night, I woke up really early feeling a strange mix of angry, embarrassed and sad. I keep replaying the argument in my head. Was I right to leave when I did? Should I have stayed and tried to work it out? What do I do now? Should I message Molly?

9.22 a.m.

Luckily, she was first to message me:

> **MOLLY:** Hey, you OK today? It was such a shame you couldn't stay. We missed you x

I really don't know what to reply. What I want to say is: *Did you see me crying? Do you like Amber more than me now? I thought you were my BFF, or doesn't that mean anything any more?*

Everything I go to type just sounds so childish.

Now I'm sitting staring at the phone, wondering what to do. I want her to know that I'm hurt but I also don't want it to end in another argument.

(10.33 a.m.)

OK, this is what I went with:

> ME: Yeh, I'm OK. I wanted to stay, but I was kind of looking forward to it being just me and you x

> MOLLY: I know you were and so was I, but Amber was on her own and it didn't seem fair to leave her out.

Note the lack of kiss.

> ME: But it was OK to leave *me* out while you two chatted about a bunch of stuff I couldn't join in with?

> MOLLY: You chose not to join in. You just sat there looking miserable all night!

ME: Because you were totally ignoring me! Can't you see what Amber's trying to do?? She's trying to take you away from me.

MOLLY: That's ridiculous. You need to stop being so jealous!

ME: I'm not jealous!

MOLLY: You are. You think it's fine for you and Jess to leave me out and go off and do stuff together, but when it comes to me making new friends you can't stand it. Amber is right – you really do need to grow up.

So she does think I'm silly and immature and she is mad about me and Jess. It looks like Amber has won – she's stolen my BFF.

Tried to talk to Mum about the Molly situation, but all she

said was: 'Can't it wait, Lottie? I've got about a million things to do before tomorrow and I'm absolutely exhausted.'

Then she asked me to look after Bella so now I'm stuck here singing that stupid Bella Smella song, which is about all anyone thinks I'm good for around here. So much for that much-needed 'quality family time', eh?

3.34 p.m.

Jess has just left. I told her what happened, and she came round dressed in her lemur onesie. She even brought lunch with her and guess what it was!

We spent the afternoon making up dance routines in our ridiculous onesies and it was totally childish **AND** silly **AND** immature yet also **SO MUCH FUN!**

I'm so lucky to have Jess in my life – I seriously don't know what I'd do without her – but I wish things were this easy with me and Molly too . . . I'm absolutely dreading school next week, but at least it's the last week before Easter. I guess I'm just going to have to keep my head down and throw myself into rehearsals.

MONDAY 4 APRIL

School was fine . . . I guess . . . if you think that your best friend since you were four totally ignoring you is fine.

It's all just so strange. We used to tell each other **EVERYTHING** and now, overnight, it's like we've become complete strangers.

Tried to talk to Mum about it again, but by the time she'd got Bella and Toby into bed she was falling asleep herself. She just never seems to have time for me any more. I wish it didn't hurt so much but it does.

TUESDAY 5 APRIL

It's Amber's birthday next month and today she brought in the invites. At first, I wasn't sure if I would be getting one, but then I remembered that leaving me out wouldn't fit in with her 'I so want me and Lottie to be friends' act.

The stack of invites was MASSIVE – she seems to have invited half of Year Seven. You should have seen them . . . They were in purple glittery envelopes tied up with turquoise ribbon and when you opened them a bunch of iridescent hearts fell out on your desk. The invite itself was on a piece of thick pink scalloped card and the details were written in gold foil. **AND it stank of Chanel No. 5** (not a hint of Poo-Pourri to be sniffed).

I was like, who does she think she is? Kim Kardashian?

I must admit it does sound pretty epic though. It's going to be a spring garden party at her house with mocktails (must remember not to drink too many!), fancy food and a proper DJ.

At first, I was like, *Well, NO WAY am I going to that*, but then I thought maybe I'll go for ten minutes or so, you know – just to check it out.

THURSDAY 7 APRIL

It was parents' evening at school tonight. Mum and Dad got back and sat me down for a 'serious chat'.

Apparently my teachers agree that I 'lack focus' and am 'prone to drifting off in class'.

Well, that's not my fault, is it?! Maybe if they made their lessons a bit more interesting, then I wouldn't have to spend my time daydreaming.

School is so boring and outdated. I mean, why do we need to do long division when you have a calculator on your phone? And why do you need to know how to spell when we have predictive text? In fact, why do we need to know anything when we can just google information as and when we need it?

It would be far better if they taught more useful stuff like how to build a substantial YouTube following or how to get TikTok-famous. That's where the money is, after all!

FRIDAY 8 APRIL

Last day of term and I can't say I wasn't relieved.

In a last-ditch attempt to try and make things right with Molly before the Easter holidays I asked if she wanted to meet for a bubble tea in town tomorrow.

She said she couldn't because she and Amber were going to the cinema with Josh and Asher. Guess it looks like they got the double date they were talking about then.

She's clearly moving on with her life, and I'm being left behind.

I don't think I'm the only one though. I saw Poppy walking through the gates alone at home time and she looked really down.

'Have a good holiday!' I called out.

'You too,' she said kindly.

I remembered that saying 'two's company, three's a crowd' and wondered if she'd been feeling left behind too.

'Hey, Poppy . . .' I started hesitantly. 'Have you tried bubble tea before?'

'Have I tried it?! **I LOVE IT!**'

'Do you fancy grabbing some over the holidays with me and Jess?'

'Really?' she said, looking dead shocked but also happy.

'Of course,' I said, smiling.

I told her I'd message her the plans and as she walked away she called back, 'Thanks, Lottie. I'm really looking forward to it.'

SATURDAY 9 APRIL

Woke up this morning feeling quite down.

Today is the day that Amber and Molly are out on their double date and I'm sitting here all alone with only my hamsters for company. (No offence intended, guys!)

What a sad, lonely life I lead.

Actually, ignore all that 'woe is me' malarky. Mum just came in and said me and her are going shopping in town. Better still, she's leaving Dad at home with Toby and Bella. Whoop! Maybe she's sensed something is wrong after all.

4.23 p.m.

Feeling happy as me and Mum had such a lovely day. I can't remember the last time I had her all to myself.

First, we went to get me measured for a new bra and, although it was a bit cringy, it was no way as embarrassing as the very first time (mostly because Toby wasn't there running around screeching and waving bras about the place).

Anyway, **DRUM ROLL** . . .

I'm now a 28A!!

So, rather than having almost completely flat triangle bits, my bra now feels like it has an actual purpose.

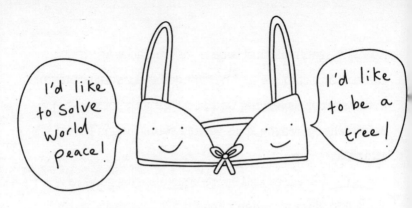

(I didn't know where to put the face on a bra . . .
it looked strange with one face so now it's got two
faces . . . and two purposes (tee hee). Just thought I'd
explain that in case it was confusing.)

It did seem like a bit of a waste of money getting new bras so soon after the first ones (it was only six months ago) but Mum said it's really important to wear bras that fit properly or you'll get a bad back. I think I'm still a long way off worrying about that though!

Mum also said that my breasts growing is a sign that my period could start soon. I really hope it does! She said that I should remember to take my period pack with me to school every day. (That's a little fabric pouch I keep in a pocket in my bag. Inside, it has a couple of sanitary towels, some wipes and spare knickers – it's good to know it's there for when I need it.)

Next, we went to Starbucks and when we'd sat down with our drinks Mum gave me a serious look and said she had something she wanted to say. I felt pretty nervous as I thought she was going to start going on about parents' evening again. Luckily, it wasn't that . . .

'Lottie, I'm sorry I haven't been there for you lately, but the truth is I've been struggling. Having three kids is a lot of work and with Bella's reflux and sleeping problems I've been so tired and stressed. I think sometimes, when you're a kid, you tend to think of your parents a bit like superheroes who can do it all, but . . . we're really not. Sometimes I don't understand how I got to be an adult with three kids because inside I still feel like I'm twelve years old, just like you. Anyway, what I'm saying in a long, rambling sort of way is that I'm sorry if I've made mistakes, but I'm only human and maybe we can both help each other a bit more?'

It felt really weird to hear my mum say that she'd been finding things hard because I had always thought of her as this really strong person who just gets on with stuff. Maybe I've been a bit wrapped up in myself too?

'I'm sorry as well, Mum,' I said. 'I've been a bit selfish lately. I promise I'll help you around the house more.'

Mum laughed. I don't think she believed me.

And then I said, 'Mum, do you really feel about twelve years old inside?'

And she said, 'Yes, I don't think you ever truly grow up inside.'

So, I said, 'Well . . . no offence, but you definitely look more like fifty.'

She looked horrified and said, 'Lottie, I'm only forty-one!'

And then we both laughed a lot.

SUNDAY 10 APRIL

Mum's made a last-minute decision that we are going to stay at Granny and Grandad's house for Easter as she says we all need a bit of a break! I think she's also looking forward to getting some help with Bella too – I don't think it helped that Bella decided to get up for the day at **3.30 A.M. EEEK!**

It'll be nice to get away for a bit, but I'm in two minds about it, so I've been making a list of the pros and cons (yes, I am a little bored).

PROS:

- ★ Granny and Grandad are much less strict than Mum and Dad.

- ★ Granny makes great Yorkshire puddings.

- ★ Grandad gives us money.

- ★ Granny gets really good junky stuff for breakfast like waffles and Pop Tarts.

* Grandad swears all the time, which
  makes Mum cross (but it makes me
  and Toby laugh).

CONS:

* Long drive.

* Grandad always watching snooker or darts on
  the telly.

* Granny always going on about how much we've
  grown.

* No Netflix.

* House smells of lavender.

* Have to share a room with Toby. ☹

The last one is the deal-breaker for me. However, I'm
packing my sleep mask and multiple pairs of earplugs to
try and drown him out.

MONDAY 11 APRIL

And we've arrived! Took seven hours to get to Leeds, thanks to Bella, who constantly needed feeding or a nappy change.

Toby was occupied with his iPad for a large chunk of the journey, but once the battery ran out he treated us to a three-hour game of disgusting 'Would you rather?' questions. I mean, imagine having to sit in the car next to this with no chance of escape . . .

It was lovely to see Granny and Grandad though! But Granny did the whole 'Oh my, look how big you've got!', which was even more mortifying than usual!

Still, Grandad gave us both a fiver and a Mars bar so it wasn't all bad.

TUESDAY 12 APRIL

I wanted to go to the cinema, but apparently the cinema isn't very sociable (why is that a bad thing?) so we went to look around Kirkstall Abbey instead, which is an old fallen-down church. Then we went to the cafe and everyone sat about drinking tea (not bubble tea, rubbish brown tea) and having a chat.

It was very boring, but it was either that or stay at home watching snooker with Grandad.

We did get to go to the gift shop though. I got a nice rainbow rubber and Toby got some slime.

I said, 'Haven't you got enough slime?!'

He said, 'Haven't you got enough rubbers?!'

Touché.

WEDNESDAY 13 APRIL

8.47 a.m.

We have only been here two nights, but already my darling little brother is driving me half-mad.

REASONS I DON'T LIKE SHARING A ROOM WITH TOBY:

* Immature

* Smells

* Picks nose

* Farts and laughs about it

* Goes to sleep too late

* Wakes up too early

* Always talking about boring stuff like Minecraft

* And disgusting stuff like poo

* Just generally won't ever shut up

* Irritating voice

Reesuns I dont like sharin a ruum with Lottie (by Toby):

* VERY BORIN

* Stairs at her fone ALL the time

* Dus RILLY smelly farts that are even wurse than mine

* Uses too mutch stinky bodey spray (to cover up the disgustin farts)

* Always finking about kissing boys (YUK)

11.34 a.m.

OMG!!!!!!!!!!!!! He's been reading my PRIVATE
PROPERTY!!!!!!! **HE'S DEAD MEAT!!!**

Also, just for the record, **I DO NOT** do 'rilly smelly farts'.
My farts smell as sweet as candyfloss, thank you very
much!

OK, maybe that's a slight exaggeration, but imagine if
you could actually fart candyfloss?! That would be epic.

Let's play 'Guess what we did this afternoon'! Was it . . . ?

A. Bowling or swimming or the cinema or anything vaguely fun at all

B. Visit another old falling-down thing

If you guessed B, you were right. Hooray!

Today's attraction was a seventeenth-century watermill. Yawn. Apparently they were the earliest source of mechanical energy. Like, who cares?!

I have another reason to add to my list . . .

Toby told me about his 'pants trick' this morning. I really wish he hadn't.

The 'pants trick' involves putting your pyjama bottoms on over your pants, so that when you get up in the morning you are already wearing pants and therefore you don't need to put new ones on.

Apparently the longest he's got away with this is three days. A fact he was incredibly proud of.

Little brothers are gross!

THURSDAY 14 APRIL

Rudely woken up at the crack of dawn by Toby desperate to tell me his latest joke . . .

What kind of bees make milk?

BOO BEES!

V tired. I can't cope with this much longer.

I said, 'Ugh, Toby, you are SO juvenile.'

Even though I do have to admit it was a pretty good joke.

4.01 p.m.

Today we went out on a 'nice walk'.

'Nice walks' are things that only adults understand.

When I walk, the purpose is to get from point A to point B. Such as home to school or home to Starbucks.

For some reason, parents think it's fun to go on absolutely massive walks for no reason whatsoever.

As a child with no rights whatsoever, you are often dragged out on these pointless missions.

On today's 'nice walk' I said to Mum, 'This is so boring! When can we go home?' which is a perfectly valid comment.

And she said, 'Look at the scenery, Lottie! Isn't it magnificent? Why would you want to go home?'

I looked around and all I could see was some hills and some fields, and I'm not being funny but I've seen plenty of hills and fields in my time.

Why are they so obsessed with looking at hills and fields? Sometimes I get scared when I think about growing up. Does it make everybody this boring?

FRIDAY 15 APRIL

Today is Good Friday.

What I don't understand is why on earth it's called 'Good Friday'?

Jesus was made to carry a cross up a big hill before being tortured and murdered – what's good about that?

I personally think it would make more sense to call it 'Bad Friday', but I guess it's a bit late in the day to rebrand it now.

I think most people are just pleased to get a day off work and go to the pub.

Went into town with Mum (AKA the Easter Bunny) to buy some Easter eggs and you should have seen the state of some people. I saw one man dancing on top of a pub table singing Elton John's 'Rocket Man' and I saw a lady being sick into her handbag.

I'm sure Jesus would have been really touched. Not.

Let it be known that I shall **NEVER** touch a drop of alcohol in my lifetime.

6.55 p.m.

Good Friday just got even worse. I now think it needs rebranding to **TERRIBLE** Friday or just **WORST DAY EVER**.

Just got off the phone to Jess, who is looking after the hammies while we are away, and Fuzzball the 3rd is extremely sick. Apparently he's just lying inside a toilet roll and hardly moving at all. Am incredibly worried! Maybe I shouldn't have called him Fuzzball the 3rd – the name is clearly cursed.

Broke the awful news to the fam and Granny says we can hold a candlelit vigil for him and say a prayer to God later, asking for his swift recovery. It sounds a really nice idea. I will write some nice words to say.

8.23 p.m

The vigil was lovely. Granny could only find birthday-cake candles, so we stuck them in hot cross buns and gathered round in prayer. Dad held a lighter up in the air like they do in concerts.

I wrote a little speech for him . . .

Dear Fuzzball,

*I'm so sorry we aren't with you in your hour of need. But we
are all thinking of you and praying you will be OK. You have
been the best hamster ever. Even better than Fuzzball One
and Two because you have never bitten me and you always
give such great fashion advice like the time you told me that I
really suited my green shorts and white T-shirt combo because
it made me look like a massive cauliflower – your favourite
snack! Anyway, please don't die! Me and the Professor need
you!*

Then we all cried and hugged. It was beautiful but
incredibly sad.

Feeling absolutely drained so going to try and sleep now.

SATURDAY 16 APRIL

TRIGGER WARNING. UPSETTING CONTENT AHEAD!

If you've grown a little fond of my hammies while
reading my diaries, then perhaps you might want to grab
a tissue for this next bit . . .

Are you ready?

OK. Well. I'm so sorry to tell you this but Fuzzball the 3rd
died in the night. Jess phoned this morning in tears. She
feels really guilty, but it's not her fault. There is nothing
she could have done. It was just his time to go.

That doesn't stop it being incredibly sad though. I hate
to think of what Professor Squeakington is going through
right now. He must be bereft. I feel so hopeless being so
far away and not being able to comfort him.

Jess has put Fuzzball's body in a shoebox and when we
get home we are going to have a proper funeral for him. I
want it to be a celebration of his life and all the amazing

things he did. Like the time he escaped and lived behind the fireplace for three days . . . and the time he managed to drag a pair of my knickers into his cage and make a bed out of them . . . and the time I put him on top of Dad's head and he did a wee on Dad's bald spot!

Well, this is a new low...

He was such a joker. I'm going to miss him so much!

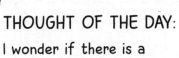

THOUGHT OF THE DAY:
I wonder if there is a
hamster heaven?

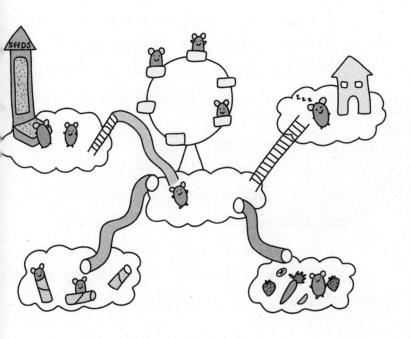

SUNDAY 17 APRIL - EASTER DAY

It's an Easter miracle!

Jess phoned first thing this morning. Fuzzball the 3rd is ALIVE! She heard scratching from the shoebox when she woke up in the morning and, sure enough, there he was nibbling at the cardboard and trying to escape.

He has risen from the dead!

I told Granny and she looked like she was going to faint. She started muttering something about 'the second coming' so I asked her what she meant, and she said it was prophesied that Jesus would return to cleanse the earth of its sins!

Anyway, Grandad made Granny a cup of tea and told her to sit in her special chair. The colour started returning to her face once she'd settled into a good episode of *A Place in the Sun*.

In other news, the Easter Bunny has been very generous this year, and me and Toby have got stacks of eggs as high as the ceiling – result! Bella isn't old enough for eggs yet, so instead she got a super-cute rabbit sleepsuit. We were all so excited to dress her up in it, but for some reason it just seemed to make her angry. Mum said she's probably teething but, honestly, nothing seems to please that girl.

Why don't you like it, Bella?

I look blimmin' ridiculous!

11.01 a.m.

Just got back from church. We don't normally go as a family but Granny's big into it.

The priest was called Father Martin and he kept making us stand up, then sit down, then kneel, then sit, then stand, kneel, sit, stand, sit, stand, kneel, etc., etc. It felt like a game of the hokey-cokey, but more boring. I was like, 'Make your mind up, mate!'

It was a bit too long IMO and there were too many songs. Loads of the people there couldn't sing at all, so it sounded absolutely awful – I thought, *If you can't beat 'em, join 'em*, so I started singing too. I must have sounded half decent because everyone started staring and clapping along with me. I felt sort of like a celeb! It made me feel a bit better about the play – it's just a shame I have to do it dressed as a weird crab.

The song I liked best was called 'Go, the Mass is Ended' because it did what it said on the tin. Everyone looked pretty relieved that it was nearly over at that point TBH.

Before we left, they asked all the kids to come forward to the altar. I was mortified because I was by far the oldest one there, but Granny made me go up anyway. I was glad in the end though, as we all got given a Creme Egg. Result.

The next thing we knew, Granny started making a beeline for Father Martin and going on about Jesus coming back as a hamster. We had to manhandle her out of the church. It took me, Mum, Dad and Grandad – she's quite strong when she wants to be!

11.53 a.m.

Granny keeps trying to slip Bella bits of chocolate. It's making Mum properly furious – it's hilarious.

To give Granny some credit, it did make the Angry Bunny Rabbit pretty happy . . . until Mum swiped the Galaxy bar out of Granny's hand and all hell broke loose.

(6.46 p.m.)

Have gone to bed with a stomach ache. Mum thought that I was old enough to be trusted to eat my Easter chocolate in moderation. She was wrong. I am clearly not ready for that responsibility yet.

This is a summary of my food intake today . . .

Breakfast: KitKat Chunky Easter egg (inc. two KitKat Chunky bars) and half a Double Decker egg (inc. one Double Decker bar).

Mid-morning snack: Fourteen Mini Eggs, one Creme Egg and the ears of a large Lindt bunny (maybe a bit of its head too).

Lunch: It was roast lamb, but I wasn't very hungry, so I just ate three Yorkshire puddings followed by two chocolate-cornflake nests, a piece of Granny's Easter cake and another Double Decker.

Afternoon snack: Two hot cross buns, two MaltEaster bunnies and two Kinder eggs. In case you are interested, one Kinder egg contained a sloth on a tree (good) and the other a speedboat (rubbish).

Dinner: Remaining body of the large Lindt bunny, remaining half of the Double Decker egg and an embarrassing amount of marshmallow chicks.

THOUGHT OF THE DAY:

What has Jesus got to do with chocolate anyway?!? I'm sure he'd be turning in his grave if he could see us all now repeatedly stuffing Lindt bunny rabbits into our gobs until we feel physically sick. To be fair though, when I die, if everyone remembered me by partaking in a day of chocolatey indulgence, I guess I'd be pretty happy. Specifically, I'd like a KitKat Chunky day – maybe they'd even sponsor it? And give everyone the day off as a public holiday. I doubt I'll ever be that important though, unless my career as a singing crustacean really takes off.

MONDAY 18 APRIL

It's boiling! It's like one of those freakishly hot spring days where it feels like it's the middle of summer.

Granny got a bit overexcited and filled up the paddling pool so that me and Toby could 'play in it'. Errr, soz, Granny, but I don't really play in paddling pools any more as I'm not five. I didn't want to hurt her feelings, so I just told her I hadn't got my swimming things with me. Her answer to that was that I should go in in my knickers!

All the adults are sitting about drinking wine in the garden. It's Mum, Dad, Grandad, Granny, Auntie Emily and Auntie Claire. Auntie Emily is married to Auntie Claire – they don't have kids; they just have loads of pets including three dogs, two cats and a massive fish tank full of tropical fish.

When I grow up, I want to be like Auntie Claire and Auntie Emily because having children looks absolutely rubbish and animals are **WAY** better than people anyway.

I once heard Mum say that she wishes she'd had pets instead of kids, which I thought was pretty rude – when I asked her about it, she insisted she was joking. Hmmmm.

Dad said Mum should be careful about how much wine she drinks because she's barely had any alcohol in the last year due to being pregnant with Bella and breastfeeding . . . I wonder if she will take any notice.

2.45 p.m.

She didn't take any notice. She was drunk after about three sips of wine.

It's now just Mum, Auntie Claire and Auntie Emily in the garden as everyone else backed off once they started cackling like a bunch of witches and using inappropriate language.

I stayed a bit longer because Mum wanted me to act out some of the play for Auntie Emily and Auntie Claire. I thought it might be a good opportunity to practise my lines, so I agreed. **BIG MISTAKE!** Now I'm worried I'm going to be a laughing stock.

Dad's taken Toby and Bella to the park and Granny and Grandad are having a 'siesta', which is a word old people use for naps to make it sound fancier than just falling asleep in front of the snooker.

I'm bored so I'm up in the bedroom practising my lines **IN PEACE** and spying on Mum, Auntie Claire and Auntie Emily from the bedroom window. They are currently singing a repertoire of Elton John songs. The lowlight was 'The Circle of Life', which sounded awful and culminated with baboon Rafiki (Mum) lifting Simba (Auntie Emily) in the air (with difficulty).

Oh God, they have stripped down to their underwear and 'gone for a swim' in the paddling pool.

Why can't I just have normal relatives?

3.44 p.m.

They are re-enacting a scene from *Jaws*. Auntie Claire
is the shark, Mum is a terrified fisherman, and Auntie
Emily is the boat.

4.02 p.m.

They are looking through old family photo albums
and crying and hugging.

They spotted me at the window and then demanded that I go out and speak to them. Then they started stroking my hair and telling me how amazing I was. Mum said, 'Having you was the best thing that ever happened to me!' and started crying (again).

Don't worry – they've cheered up again.

Dad, Bella and Toby are back, and now we are all staring agog as they perform a dance called the Macarena. If you've not heard of the song before, it's an old people's dance from last century – perhaps ask your parents to demonstrate it to you?

Sorry . . . DO NOT do that!

No one needs to see their parents doing the Macarena. Especially in their underwear.

It will scar you for life. Trust me, I know.

6.37 p.m.

EMERGENCY! EMERGENCY! Mum has downloaded TikTok!

She wants me to film them doing their semi-clad dancing and upload it – **OMG!!!!!!**

I've tried explaining that they are **WAY TOO OLD** to be on TikTok, but they are having none of it!

Apparently they think their dancing is so good that it'll go viral!!! Are they deluded?!?

Phew – crisis averted. I have hidden her phone in a flowerpot.

You may think that a bit harsh, but personally I think everyone over the age of thirty should be banned from social media.

7.12 p.m.

The party is over! Mum has 'done her back in' dancing to 'Gangnam Style'.

Auntie Emily and Auntie Claire have gone home. Dad had to give them a good telling-off and then help carry Mum indoors.

Hopefully, this will be a lesson learnt for them all!

THOUGHT OF THE DAY:
I am NEVER drinking alcohol.

TUESDAY 19 APRIL

8.33 a.m.

Today we had to get up mega early to pack our things as we are off home. There was one problem – Mum was proving very difficult to wake as she was hungover and set on having a pity party for one in bed.

Dad said he had a great idea. He grabbed a saucepan and spoon, gave Toby Grandad's old harmonica and instructed me to go and get the Angry Bunny and meet them upstairs.

I must admit we did make a rather good alarm clock and it certainly did the job – I've never seen Mum shoot out of bed so quickly!

I'm looking forward to getting back to my own bed, but I will miss everyone. It is always good fun staying here, despite the carnage, and the boring trips to old falling-down things.

CANNOT wait to see my hammies.

3.24 p.m.

Just got home. It was a hideous journey. The traffic was really bad, so Dad decided to take some country lanes instead. They were really twisty-turny and I suddenly felt really carsick and knew I was about to throw up. Mum has no sick bags in the car and we were nowhere near a service station. The only thing we could find was an old Happy Meal box on the car floor. Did a massive puke into it, but some of it dribbled out of the folds on to my jeans.

It absolutely stank! Then because the whole car smelt of puke Toby said he started feeling sick. Before any of us could find another vomit receptacle, he just puked all over himself and some of it even came out of his nose. **MINGING.**

Next Bella wakes up from her nap because of all the commotion and pukes up all over herself too.

So, there we all were, sitting in the back of the car covered in sick. Lovely.

Mum said to Dad, 'Remind me again why we chose to have children?'

Dad said, 'It was YOUR idea. I'd have been quite happy with a dog!'

CHARMING!

Then Toby spent the rest of the journey begging Mum and Dad for a dog.

He said he wanted to call it Batman or Fun Pants. I said that those were stupid names for a dog and, if we ever did get a dog, we'd call it something sensible like Penelope Wigglebutt.

Dad said he'd like to call it Nigel or Gary. To be honest, I thought those were worse than Toby's suggestions.

I asked Mum what she'd like to call the dog and she said
she'd like to call it 'Nothing because it doesn't exist and
it's NEVER happening!' – I mean, it's a bit long-winded
but it's certainly original!

Right, off for a shower to wash this yucky sick smell
away before Jess comes round in about an hour to drop
my hammies off – can't wait!

5.12 p.m.

They're back! It was so good to see them. I think they
were glad to see me too (or else they were excited about

the yoghurt drops I got them as a welcome-home present –
it's hard to say for sure).

It was also great to see Jess. I hadn't realized just how
much I'd missed her. Adorably, she had spent the holidays
trying to teach the hammies to jump through a hoop. To
be honest, I'm not sure it was exactly time well spent, but
it certainly made me laugh . . .

Fuzzball was looking pretty much back to normal, but I thought it might be best to get him checked out anyway, so I got Mum to book an emergency appointment at the vet's.

In other news, it took poor old Dad two hours to scrub all the sick out of the car seats. After he'd finished, he looked quite pale and I thought he might start vomming up himself!

WEDNESDAY 20 APRIL

Good news – the vet says that Fuzzball is absolutely
fine! The most likely scenario was that he went into a
temporary state of hibernation after overindulging in his
seed mix. He's always been a bit of a greedy guts.

Dad wasn't fine when he got hit with the bill though –
because it was an emergency consultation, it cost £35!
He said it was outrageous considering it only cost £7.50
to buy Fuzzball in the first place.

FYI: Fuzzball is not replaceable. Dad also needs to brush up on his maths skills because £35 divided by £7.50 is actually four and two thirds' worth of hamsters. Although TBH not sure what you'd do with two thirds of a hamster. **GROSS**.

THURSDAY 21 APRIL

Met up with Poppy and Jess and we went to get bubble teas. They were even yummier than last time!

Chatted to Poppy about the whole Amber situ and she said that she feels like she's been sidelined too. Apparently it's not the first time Amber's done this sort of thing, either. She seems to dump friends pretty regularly.

I asked Poppy why she's put up with it for so long, and she says she doesn't know and that Amber just has this way of making you do what she wants. Don't we all know it!

As we were finishing up our drinks, she turned to me and Jess and said, 'You guys have been so nice to me and I feel terrible that I've been mean to you in the past. So I just wanted to say . . . I'm really sorry.'

'That's OK,' said Jess. 'I get it.'

'Yeh, me too – and the most important thing is that we are friends now, right?' I said.

Poppy smiled. 'Right.'

After leaving the bubble-tea shop, we realized we didn't have any money left, so we did what we usually do when we run out of cash – sat in the park and stared at people.

We'd only been there a few minutes and guess who appeared . . . Beautiful Theo and Wotsit Fingers!

I panicked and decided that the best thing to do would be to hide behind a tree.

I watched as they came over and started chatting to Jess and Poppy.

Poppy goes to Wotsit Fingers, 'Are you not with Marnie?'

And he goes, 'Didn't you hear? We split up . . .'

Behind the tree, I'm like **OMG!!!!!!!!!!!!!!!!!!!!!!!**

'How come?'

'Basically, we were incompatible. Her favourite crisps are cheese and onion . . .'

Jess goes, 'Urgh, whose favourite crisps are cheese and onion?!'

'Yeh. It was a deal-breaker for me. I mean cheese is good and pickled onion is good, but cheese and onion together?! Nah – it was never going to work.'

He makes a very good point, because if you don't like the same flavours of crisps, then what hope has your relationship got?

'Are you guys seeing Lottie today?'

OOOOH this was getting interesting . . .

'Um . . . we . . . yeh . . . she should be meeting us here . . .' said Poppy.

'Is she here already because it looks like she's trying to hide behind that tree over there,' said Theo.

STUPID TOO-SMALL TREE!

At this point I had no choice but to reveal myself.

'Why are you looking at a tree?!' asked Wotsit Fingers.

'I was just, um . . . I like trees so . . . I just like to . . . look at them . . . quite closely.'

'And how did it look?'

'Quite . . . nice and barky . . . I guess . . .'

And then Daniel started laughing, which gave me the giggles too.

Then we talked about trees, and school and the play and crisps, and it turns out he loves Monster Munch! It was probably the most successful conversation we've ever had.

As we left, he said, 'Are you going to Amber's party next weekend?'

And I said, 'Yeh.'

And he said, 'See you there?'

And I said, 'Cool.'

SQUEEEEEAAALLLLLLLLLLLLLLLLLLLLLLLLLLLL!

SATURDAY 23 APRIL

Should really have been doing my homework, but Jess came round and we spent four hours absolutely nailing (IMO) a TikTok dance routine instead.

The really annoying thing was that it only got three likes.

Felt like a wasted day!

SUNDAY 24 APRIL

I'm feeling kind of anxious about going back to school tomorrow because things are still really weird between me and Molly. Usually over the school holidays we'd have spent loads of time together and we'd have been constantly messaging each other when I was away in Leeds.

This time round, apart from the odd like on Instagram or TikTok, we've not spoken and, if I'm being completely honest, I miss her. I miss her a lot.

I keep thinking about all the things we've done together in the past. It just feels so sad that our friendship might be over. She's been part of my life for so long that I can't even remember not knowing her.

Mum could see I was struggling and she came up to my room to talk to me.

'You don't seem yourself today, Lottie . . . What's wrong, love?'

'I feel like I'm losing Molly,' I said, and then I started crying.

'Oh, darling, I'm sorry to hear that. You and Molly have been best friends for so long it must be very difficult. But, as you grow older, people change – and, although it can be hard, sometimes the best thing to do is to give them a bit of space . . . You see, friendships aren't something you can force . . .'

I gave her a big hug; I knew she was right.

Molly thinks I'm just jealous and can't handle her having other friends (and that might be a tiny bit true) but one thing is for sure – the more I try to talk to her about it, the worse it gets. So I need to take a step back and let her work it out for herself, because all I'm doing at the minute is pushing us further apart.

I also need to try and focus big time on the play as there are only four days left to go. **SCARED**.

We also have our first official dress rehearsal tomorrow!

Singing crustacean day !!!

MONDAY 25 APRIL

Things were fine with Molly today. Well, not as bad as they could have been anyway. We didn't hug or chat or hang out like we usually would, but at least we weren't totally ignoring each other either. We smiled and said hi and left it at that. I feel much better about it all after the chat with Mum yesterday.

In the afternoon, everyone in the play got to miss classes for the dress rehearsal – result.

As we walked into the auditorium, me and Jess were like **WOW!** The set had been installed over Easter and it looked amazing. There were streams of blue and green crêpe paper hanging from the rafters, big rocks, coral and shells made from papier mâché, beautiful purple lighting, and the sound of waves and seagulls playing through the sound system. It actually felt like you were under the sea!

Mrs Lane gathered us round and started handing out costumes, which were mostly made by parents with a talent for sewing. Mine had a padded shell body and eight legs, which were made from red tights stuffed with newspaper. I have two big cardboard claws that go on a bit like gloves and a headband with straws attached with ping-pong balls on top for eyes. I look incredible and completely ridiculous at the same time.

Jess doesn't look ridiculous at all. She's wearing the most beautiful fish-tailed cocktail dress you ever did see!

Jess looking ultra glam

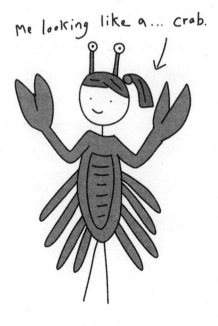

Me looking like a... crab.

The run-through went pretty well, until the finale, that is. I was getting so into the part, singing loudly and scuttling along sideways (as crabs do), that I failed to notice that I was approaching the edge of the stage and I went absolutely flying.

Luckily, the newspaper in my (fake) legs seemed to cushion my fall as, apart from a few bruises, I escaped pretty lightly. Now I'm just hoping that doesn't happen in three days' time when I'm up there in front of all those people.

TUESDAY 26 APRIL

Well, you'll be pleased to hear that I didn't fall off the stage again today. However, before you breathe a sigh of relief, you should be aware that something **EVEN** worse happened.

Mrs Lane was trying to repair a part of Jess's costume that had come loose at the seams, and she said to me, 'Lottie, would you mind popping to reception and asking to borrow a pair of scissors, please?'

I said, 'But, miss – I'm dressed as a crab!'

'I'm sure they won't mind, Lottie,' she replied.

'Yes, but, miss, it's just that I –'

'Lottie, I'm incredibly busy right now and I'd really appreciate it if you could just do as I ask.'

'OK, miss,' I said reluctantly. She was pretty stressed and I didn't feel brave enough to keep arguing my case.

I contemplated taking the costume off, but, seeing as it takes me about fifteen minutes to get in and out of it, that wasn't really an option either. I looked at the clock and sighed – there were three minutes until the end of school, when the corridors would fill with pupils. Could I make it to reception and back in time?! Only one way to find out.

GO, LOTTIE, GO!

I ran to reception as fast as I could. Which wasn't actually very fast, because for some stupid reason I did it sideways (again). I just keep forgetting that I'm not actually a crab! DOH. It also reduced my visibility of oncoming hazards, so I totally missed the CAUTION – SLIPPERY FLOOR sign that the school uses after mopping up random kid vomit (which happens on a frighteningly frequent basis).

WHOOOOOOOOOSH! I went absolutely flying head first. Those shiny school floors are incredibly skiddy when wet. Luckily, the stuffed tights took the brunt of the fall again, but my headband was knocked out of place and I watched as one of my eyeballs bounced off down the hall.

At that exact moment, as if on cue, I heard the worst sound you could imagine.

RIIIIIIIIIIINNNNNNNNNG!

Yup. The school bell, signalling the end of the day.

There was nothing else to do but lie in a puddle and await my fate.

In the sea of legs, I lost sight of my eyeball. I started to panic. Mrs Lane was stressed enough already; I couldn't come back minus an eyeball.

But what is this?!

Suddenly, before me, a knight in shining armour appears. It's Daniel! He's on his knees and looks a bit like he is about to propose to me. All my dreams have come true!

EXCEPT instead of a ring he is offering me a ping-pong ball. But details . . . details . . .

I went bright red, which was fine as I was ninety-five per cent red already, so the blush blended in quite well.

I thanked Daniel, went to collect the scissors and ran back to rehearsal. Job done.

THOUGHT OF THE DAY:
Although it was quite exciting almost to be proposed to, I'm kind of glad it didn't happen like that. I'd prefer *something* slightly more romantic. Also, one-eyed crab lying in a pool of vomity water isn't exactly my best look.

WEDNESDAY 27 APRIL

This morning Mr Peters was like, 'Miss Brooks, I don't seem to have your maths homework.'

I was like, 'Are you for real, sir?! I'm a famous West End star now. I don't have time for working out the volume of a cuboid!'

In my head anyway. In actual life I said, 'Oops, sorry, sir,' and **THEN** he cruelly gave me lunchtime detention and made me stay in and do it.

Honestly, all the time and effort I dedicate to this school and that's the thanks I get!

There were no rehearsals today as Mrs Lane said she wanted everybody well rested and relaxed for tomorrow night. Is she insane? . . . How on earth are we meant to relax?!

I mean, what if I forget all my lines? What if I freak out and my words don't come out right? What if I sing horrendously off-key? What if I accidentally forget to put my costume on and walk out on stage completely naked?!?!? (Not quite sure exactly how that would ever happen, but still.)

Mum suggested I download a mindfulness app on my phone and then listen to it in my room to help calm myself down.

It didn't exactly work though . . .

close your eyes and relax... imagine you are by the Sea... imagine the birds are tweeting ... imagine the waves gently crashing... I MAGINE you WEE youR PANTS ON STAGE!

THURSDAY 28 APRIL

ARGHHHHHHHH IT'S TODAY!!!!!!!!

Didn't sleep very well at all last night, thanks to that
stupid app. I had a dream that I did actually wee my
pants on stage. Like, literally in front of everyone – it
was horrific . . .

So now, to add to my 'naked on stage' paranoia, I also have an 'I might wee on stage' paranoia. Fantastic.

Mental reminder: I **MUST** go to the toilet four times before the show and also keep checking my body to make sure it's got clothes on.

Wish me luck!

10.37 p.m

I should be trying to get to sleep but I can't as so much has happened and I just **NEED** to tell you **ASAP**.

Firstly, you will be relieved to know that I didn't go out on stage naked or do a wee on it. **YAY! GO, ME!**

However, it didn't exactly all go to plan either (does my life ever??) . . .

Anyway, there I am, in the wings dressed in full costume and I can hear the auditorium filling with **HUNDREDS** of people. I start feeling dead nervous as I imagine Mum,

Dad, Toby and Bella taking their seats near the front. (They were arriving early to make sure they got good ones.)

Suddenly I started to worry that I needed the toilet again. I'd already been three times, but that stupid dream was making me think I needed to make a fourth trip. I looked at my watch. I had fifteen minutes; I could make it if I hurried. I decided to make a dash for it.

As I've mentioned though, I was now in full costume, and you won't be surprised to hear that going to the toilet wasn't the easiest of jobs . . . I mean, I had eight legs, ten if you included my actual human legs and twelve if you included my pincers – that's a whole lot of legs to fit inside a toilet cubicle! I managed to declaw myself and pull the shell construction up over my hips and sit on the toilet. I started to wee. That's when I noticed it – there was blood in my knickers.

I know starting my period is something that I've been thinking about for ages, but I still felt so shocked that it had actually happened. It wasn't how I'd imagined at all. Not like this . . . Certainly not dressed as a large crab that was due on stage in about ten minutes. Then I realized I didn't have my bag with me, so my period pack was backstage, and I had no way of getting it in time.

I started to panic – what on earth was I going to do? I couldn't help it. I burst into tears.

Then I heard the toilet door swing open, so I tried to stop crying and stay as quiet as I could. But the footsteps were coming my way. Someone came walking along outside the stalls . . .

'Lottie, are you in here?'

I let out a big sob. Mostly through relief at hearing the voice that I so needed right then.

'Molly?'

'What's wrong? Are you crying? I saw you dash off and I was worried . . .'

'I . . . I . . . think I've started my . . . period.'

'Oh, Lottie! Do you have sanitary towels?'

'No . . . I've left my bag backstage . . . I don't know what to do!'

'OK, don't worry. Stay right there – I'll go and find your bag. I'll be back in two minutes, I promise.'

So I did stay there. I mean, I didn't have a huge amount of choice, did I?

When she got back, she passed me my bag under the door and I managed to change my underwear and stick the towel in place. Big relief!

As I was coming out of the cubicle, Amber came running in.

'Molly, Lottie – everyone is looking for you! Curtains go up in five – come on!'

'I don't know if I can,' I said. I was still feeling quite shaken up and the last thing I felt like doing was going out there in front of all those people.

Amber looked confused, but then a look of understanding spread across her face. Could she tell? Can people just tell when you have your period?

'Lottie, you can! We need you,' said Molly. 'And I know I've never said this before, but your performance of "Under the Sea" is . . . it's just brilliant.'

Amber nodded her head enthusiastically. 'Come on – you **CAN** do this!'

What was going on – even Amber was being kind of nice to me?

I knew they were right. I'd been preparing for this moment for weeks. I knew my lines and lyrics like the back of my hand. (BTW why do people say that? I don't even know if I **DO** know the back of my hand that well. I mean, it's just a hand, right? And it looks like plenty of other people's hands!)

'OK. Let's go!' I said, before I could change my mind.

We got backstage just as the performance was about to begin. Mrs Lane looked stressed; she was pacing around and rubbing her forehead. When she saw us come back in, she looked **VERY** relieved.

'Come on, girls! Get into place quickly!'

I didn't need to be on for the first few minutes so I watched from the wings and, although I could feel the nerves inside my tummy, they didn't feel like bad doubting nerves – they felt like an energy that I needed to get out.

Then suddenly it was my cue. I scurried sideways on stage. The audience was in darkness so I just pretended that they weren't there. I delivered my lines clearly and loudly, much better than I've ever done in rehearsals, and when it was my time to sing I actually enjoyed it. I could hear people clapping, laughing and singing along, so I assumed they were enjoying it too.

I was having so much fun that I didn't want it to be over. It felt like it went far too quickly. After the finale aquarium date (which people **LOVED**) the lights came up and we all came back on stage and took big bows to a standing ovation! I saw my whole family clapping wildly in the front row and I even caught a glimpse of Daniel in the third row with his parents and brother and he was clapping and grinning at me too.

As for Jess, she absolutely stole the show. Her performance of 'Part of Your World' was nothing short of mesmerizing – wow, that girl can really sing. When we came off stage, I told her she was going to be a famous movie star someday – but she said she doesn't want to be a movie star, or a mermaid, or a princess. She wants to be a forensic scientist – which is exactly why she's so awesome!

After we'd got changed, it was time to meet the fans, and when I saw Mum and Dad in the foyer they dashed right over and told me they were so proud. Even Toby said I was 'pretty good' and Bella, bless her, did a smelly sicky burp and gave me a big gummy smile.

It was pretty late by the time we got home, but while Mum got Bella and Toby to bed I waited up for her. In all the excitement I had almost forgotten about today's **MAJOR** development, but I couldn't go to sleep without telling her first.

I mean, as you can probably guess, she cried and did way too much of the whole 'journey into womanhood' thing and I did the whole '**Muuuuuuuuuuuuum**, you're so embarrassing!' and rolling-my-eyes thing. But she was pretty great – I think I'll keep her.

So yeh, all in all it was a pretty eventful night! Must go to bed now. I'm absolutely shattered.

FRIDAY 29 APRIL

Woke up . . . remembered . . . took a shower . . . put my underwear on . . . with a new sanitary towel! I have a small tummy ache, but it's not so bad. I'm sure the appeal will wear off, but for now it feels strange, though in a good way. I don't know why but I feel kind of invincible.

School was brilliant because me and Jess found out what it was like to be famous – well, sort of. Even some of the Year Eights seem to know our names now and so many people came up to congratulate me for being a brilliant crab. There's a sentence I thought I'd never hear in my life!

Things with Molly and Amber are . . . not sure how I'd say it . . . fine? I guess. I'm super grateful to Molly for being there for me yesterday, but today it's still very much her and Amber again.

I don't know how things will work out in the future, but I hope we'll always be friends, even if we aren't as close as we used to be.

Don't get me wrong – I'd love to tell you that there was a perfect, happy ending, the kind you do get in Disney movies. But life doesn't always work out that way, and I think I'm getting used to that.

A bit.

SATURDAY 30 APRIL – AMBER'S PARTY

AKA the worst day ever.

Woke up this morning to bright sunshine. I guess even the weather wouldn't dare try and put a dampener on Amber's birthday party, huh?

I feel a mix of nervous and excited – mostly because going to a boy/girl party is about the most adult thing I've ever done. I'm not counting the ones I went to when I was five BTW – I don't think there will be Pass the Parcel or Pin the Tail on the Donkey, which is a shame as I really love party games.

The only problem is that, because I've been so focused on the play, I've not given my outfit choice much thought at all. And by *much*, I mean any.

I've looked at every item of clothing in my wardrobe and nothing was right for a spring garden party.

Or should I say a spring garden party **WITH BOYS**.

Or should I say a spring garden party **WITH THE BOY
I'M IN 'LIKE' WITH**.

Argh. I need to get a grip. I need someone to hit me round
the face with a wet fish.

10.45 a.m.

I couldn't find any wet fish, only fish fingers. I asked Toby
to assist and he loved the idea . . .

. . . perhaps a bit too much. He lobbed an entire pack at me!

Enough! I needed to focus. There were only six hours left to go until the party!

I went back upstairs and emptied my entire wardrobe on to the floor, which wasn't at all helpful, but it did make a nice place to lie down and feel sorry for myself.

I shouted down to Mum to let her know about my predicament.

She came up to my room and started going through the pile. 'You've got loads of lovely things here . . . How about this?' she said while holding up a white dress covered in roses with a pink net skirt and bow tied at the waist. 'You used to love this one! Do you remember you used to wear it with those pink glittery slip-on shoes and one of my old handbags?'

'**OMG, MUM!** I used to love that when I was about seven. If I wore that to the party, I'd get laughed at so badly I'd have to change schools and possibly even continents.'

She has absolutely zero clue.

(11.37 a.m.)

Decided to focus on perfecting my make-up instead.

If I don't have anything nice to wear, maybe I can distract people with my on-fleek eyeliner.

However, it's much harder than it looks. I did one side OKish, but then I did the other side and that side was thicker. So, I corrected the first side and then that side was thicker. Then I topped up the other side to even it out, but it went all wonky, so I had to thicken it up even more. Then I had to thicken the first side too. This went on and on and on until I ended up looking like a very angry panda.

Why is it so hard to do that cute, flicked eyeliner properly?! Operating liquid eyeliner is another thing they should teach at GCSE!

WhatsApp conversation with Liv:

> **ME:** URGENT! I need to look good for a party today. All my clothes make me look like a potato and I tried to do my eyeliner, but I ended up looking like this:

LIV: 🤣 🤣 🤣

ME: Stop laughing! I don't want to look like a potato/angry panda hybrid thing. I want to look nice!

LIV: Sorry! Makeovers are my speciality. Come over ASAP!

2.05 p.m.

EEEK, that was amazing. I owe Liv like a million pounds. Or maybe just a tenner or something . . .

First, we went through her wardrobe and found a bunch of stuff that she had grown out of. I tried on a couple of dresses, some jean shorts and tops that were all much better than anything I had at home, but eventually we decided on a denim playsuit. It's so cute – I love it!

I also decided that it might be the right occasion to de-hair my legs for the first time (I don't really count the time I hacked away at them with Dad's razor). Liv showed me how to apply the hair-removing cream (it only took a few minutes) and then, when I washed it off, my legs were so silky smooth I couldn't stop touching them. I borrowed some tinted body moisturizer too, to give them a nice sun-kissed glow.

Next, she did my make-up and nailed the winged eyeliner first time (wow). She curled my eyelashes with one of those weird contraption things and applied black mascara, then she finished the look with some bronzer on my cheeks and a light pink lip gloss, which looks great with the blue denim.

Time for hair. As you will probably know, I very rarely

do anything different with my hair apart from put it in a high pony, but Liv said it would be nice to do some gentle waves, so she quickly got to work with her curling wand.

'Right, I think you are done, Lottie! Do you want to see yourself?' she said as she finished me off with some hairspray.

'I guess so,' I replied nervously.

I mean, what if I looked completely stupid?

But I shouldn't have worried because OMG look at the transformation . . .

When I got back home, Dad said, 'Who are you and what have you done with our daughter?' which was obviously totally hilarious. Not.

Mum looked like she was about to cry (yes again). She said, 'Oh gosh, I can't believe our baby is off to her first proper party!'

Even Toby said I looked OK for a girl, whatever that is supposed to mean.

Anyway, now I'm just twiddling my lovely hair and waiting for Jess and Poppy to arrive to pick me up.

I can't stop looking at myself in the mirror. I mean, I know looks aren't everything, yada, yada, yada, but I barely recognize myself and it's **SOOOO** nice to feel glammed up for once.

Oh gosh, I have such a nervous tummy!

8.34 p.m.

Guess who's back! **ME**.

Can you guess what happened? Nah.

Do you want me to tell you? That's a rhetorical question, because I'm going to tell you anyway and if your answer was no, then how rude are you?!

For those of you who are interested, here is the party low-down . . .

We arrived fashionably late and the party was already in full swing. Jess was wearing a neon-green mini dress that only she could pull off and Poppy had gone for a more sophisticated LBD. Everyone was very complimentary about our outfits. People kept coming up to me and going **'OMG, LOTTIE! YOU LOOK AMAZEBALLS!'** and doing double takes and stuff. It was clearly a much better look for me than the crab costume.

Amber looked incredible, but maybe slightly **OTT** in a full-on prom dress and high-heeled sandals. She was stomping about the place with a face like thunder.

I was really relieved when Molly came over to say

hi to us. She said I looked great and that she barely recognized me at first.

'What's wrong with Amber?' I asked her.

'What makes you think something's wrong with her?' said Jess.

'Have you seen her face?'

Amber's angry face*

*It was even worse IRL.

'Asher and Josh haven't turned up,' explained Molly. 'They cancelled last minute and apparently they've been posting stories on Instagram at a party of another Year Eight kid.'

'Ouch.'

'Yeh, I know. I'm OK, but I think Amber's taken it quite badly.'

I mean, I'm no fan of Amber's, but it's pretty harsh to get blown out on your birthday like that.

We went to check out the rest of the party, and the decorations were amazing. Amber's mum and dad must have spent an absolute fortune on helium balloons because they were everywhere. There were big twelve-shaped balloons, heart-shaped balloons, balloons filled with glitter and feathers, and a few random ones like hamburgers, watermelon slices and ice lollies.

Instead of just having all the food and drinks on the table like you usually get at parties, there were actual waiters dressed in waistcoats walking around with trays full of mocktails and hoor derves (not sure how you spell that word, but you know what I mean . . . posh snacks on a tray). I thought, *Wow! This is what it must feel like to be a* **PROPER ADULT.** (Without any of the rubbish bits like getting obsessed with hanging your towel up after a shower instead of leaving it in a heap on the bed. Like, seriously, why do old people get so boring?! Yawn.)

Me and Jess and Poppy hatched a plan to stand next to the kitchen where all the food was coming out so that we could stuff our faces with all the best stuff. It was all **SO YUM!** There were tiny cones of chips, little pieces of toast with fancy ham on, chicken on a stick with peanut sauce, and the absolute star of the show – miniature cheeseburgers.

Jess said, 'I know, Lottie. Why don't you see how many you can fit in your mouth at once?'

Poppy said, 'OMG, Lottie! No, you can't do that at a party!' but she was also laughing hysterically, which TBH spurred me on because I can never say no to a challenge.

Guess how many I managed – five!!! The girls were dead impressed.

I was feeling really pleased with myself until Daniel appeared from absolutely nowhere.

I was so annoyed. On the one night I'd actually glammed myself up!

Daniel looking cute   Me with 5 burgers in my gob

He seemed dead shy and kept staring at his feet, but for once in my life I didn't feel that nervous in front of him . . . which was annoying as I had my mouth stuffed full of miniature burgers.

He said, 'Hi, Lottie, you look really . . . um . . . you look really great.'

And I said, 'Mmm, fanf fooo Faniel.'

'It's a great party, huh?'

'Mmm, mrate mrartey.'

'And the cheeseburgers are pretty good too, aren't they?'

'Mrh . . . mrilly mrummy.'

At which point Jess and Poppy lost the plot and started to giggle uncontrollably. I couldn't help but start to laugh too – but, as my mouth was still full of burgers, I also started to choke. Daniel gave me a big slap on the back and the next thing I knew I did a big cough/ sneeze at the same time and the congealed burger-ball shot halfway across the room (probably along with a good teaspoon full of my snot/phlegm).

I was mortified. Why does this sort of thing always seem to happen to me??

Daniel looked worried. 'Are you OK?' he said.

I tried to act dead casual about it all. 'Yeh, fine. I just think those things are a bit difficult to chew, that's all.'

Jess said, 'It may also be the fact that she ate five at once.'

THANKS, JESS.

Next thing we knew we heard Theo shout . . .

And we all burst out laughing. Daniel included. As weird and awkward as it was, I think at last I'm starting to be able to be myself around him.

Back in the snug, Amber had gathered everyone round. I assumed she was going to make some sort of cringey speech, but instead she said, 'Now we are going to play Truth or Dare. Everyone, get in a circle please!'

My heart sank as I **HATE** Truth or Dare. I can embarrass myself enough in my day-to-day life; I certainly don't need any help from a stupid game.

Everyone sat down and we started to play: you had to choose whether you wanted to answer a truth or do a dare, and then people randomly shouted out the questions and tasks.

Jacinta had to eat a spoonful of garlic puree (minging), Ben had to let us write **IDIOT** on his head in a black Sharpie (fitting), Louis said he'd kissed three girls before (probably a lie), Mia admitted to having a crush on Mr Peters (ewwwww) and Kylie had to run round the garden five times shouting 'HELP! I'M A TOMATO

AND THEY ARE TRYING TO TURN ME INTO KETCHUP!'
(just bizarre).

When it was Amber's turn, she chose dare.

'Jump in the hot tub with your clothes on!' shouted
Ben.

'What! Do you know how much this dress cost? I'm
not doing that one – pick another.'

'You can't just pick another one,' he said.

'It's my party and I can do what I like!'

No one had the energy to argue.

She nudged Kylie and whispered something to her. You
could tell whatever it was that Kylie was not too happy
about it.

'I dare Amber . . . ' she began nervously, '. . . to kiss
Theo.'

Amber made a big show of acting dead shocked, like she hadn't just directly told Kylie to say that.

Theo didn't look best pleased, either, as she made her way across the room to him.

'Just on the cheek,' he said.

She was absolutely gutted!

Next it was Theo's turn – he chose truth and Amber asked him, 'Out of everyone at the party, who do you most fancy?'

I assume she was really hoping he would say her. But he didn't. He looked around the room, blushed a little and said, 'Molly.'

Everyone started cheering and, although Amber was trying to appear casual about it, you could see the rage brewing behind her fake smile. Molly was going to be in serious hot water with her later.

Next, Daniel said truth and Molly asked him a similar

question: 'If you could ask anyone here out, who would it be?'

I looked down at the floor, willing it to be over. I didn't want to know.

After what felt like a million years, he said . . .

um... Lottie

'Oh, look how red she's going!' shouted Amber. 'It must be love!'

I **HATE** it when people do that. I looked at my watch. Dad would be coming to pick me and Jess up soon.

I wished he'd hurry up. I really REALLY didn't want to play any longer.

'Lottie! Your turn,' I heard Amber say.

DAMMIT.

I chose dare, as I'd much rather do something stupid like jump into the hot tub than admit to the entire party that I had a crush on Daniel.

'Hmmm,' said Amber with a look on her face that I didn't like at all. 'I dare you to kiss Daniel . . . on the lips!'

What?! I couldn't believe it. I was fuming at Amber. Why does she always try her hardest to embarrass me?

Jess grabbed my hand. 'You don't have to do it, Lottie. It's just a stupid game. Everyone can see she's just trying to get a reaction.'

I didn't want to kiss Daniel. Well, maybe I did . . . one day.

But not right there, as part of a game in front of a big group of people.

I stood up. 'Great party, Amber, but we've got to go.'

'What? You can't just leave like –'

'Yeh, we can. Later, Amber!' said Jess, jumping to her feet too.

Amber looked angry enough to burst. But it was her own fault.

I shot an apologetic look at Daniel as we left, none of it was his fault.

So yeh, all in all it was fun . . . but also a bit weird. I feel proud of myself though for having the confidence to walk out.

And there were also some good bits too. I spoke to Daniel like a semi-normal human being **AND** he **PICKED ME!!!** I just hope I haven't given him the wrong impression by leaving like that.

DANIEL: Hope you are OK. Everyone could see what Amber was trying to do. Well done for standing up to her! x

A kiss!!!! OMG!!!!!!!!!!!!! I composed a casual reply.

ME: Thanks. I'm good. How was the rest of the party? x

DANIEL: Not great. Theo and Molly ended up chatting quite a bit and Amber started stomping round the place like a jealous kid.

ME: LOL. Yeh, I bet that went down well. Glad we left when we did then.

DANIEL: Yeh, it was a good decision.

I thought – is that it?!?! But then I saw the dots start to move – Daniel is typing something . . .

HURRY UP THEN, DANIEL. DON'T LEAVE ME
HANGING LIKE THIS!

DANIEL: I wanted to ask you something
tonight, but I always chicken out when I
see you...

Say what?! **HE** gets nervous around **ME?!?**

DANIEL: *Typing...*

I CAN'T TAKE IT ANY MORE! ASK ME,
DANIEL, ASK ME!!

DANIEL: I mean you can say no, obvs.

I CAN SAY NO TO WHAT, DANIEL?!?!

DANIEL: Would you like to go get an
ice cream with me sometime?

So, I'm all like . . .

OMG!!!!!!!
WHAT. IS. GOING. ON
I CAN'T BREATHE!
How does breathing
work again?!

Luckily, I remembered how to breathe because otherwise there would be a slightly more tragic ending to this story.

I waited a minute or two until the urge to message back **'YES! YES! YES!'** had passed and then I replied with . . .

> **ME:** Yeh, that'd be cool. I love ice cream!

> **DANIEL:** Great. How about next Saturday? And me too. What's your favourite flavour? I'm torn between chocolate fudge and salted caramel.

> **ME:** Mint choc chip all the way . . .
> or lemon sorbet on a really hot
> day! PS I've checked the calendar
> and I think I can squeeze you in
> the Saturday after next 😊

And then we proceeded to spend about half an hour debating ice-cream flavours – it was perfect.

Before we said goodnight, he had one more thing to ask me . . .

> **DANIEL:** Oh, BTW . . . was the card you
> sent to Dan the Man really for me?

Dear reader, I **CRINGED** when he asked me that, but what else could I do but come clean?

> **ME:** I mean, I hate to admit it.
> But yeh. It was.

> **DANIEL:** And do you really like me more
> than a KitKat Chunky?

ME: Are you insane? Of course not.

DANIEL:

THOUGHT OF THE DAY:
I'VE GOT A BOYFRIEND AND I'M IN LOVE.
No, stop it! Must stay calm. I'm going on
a date with a boy I like. No need to get
overexcited.

SUNDAY 1 MAY

Woke up today feeling fifty per cent happy (Daniel related) and fifty per cent sad (Molly related) and by weird coincidence, just as I was thinking of sending her a text, Molly's name popped up on FaceTime on my phone.

I rolled over in bed and accepted the call.

She looked nervous. 'I miss you so much,' she said.

I couldn't help it – I burst into tears. 'Not as much as I miss you!'

And then she was crying too.

'I know Amber can be a bit . . . difficult . . . but I don't want her to come between us . . . She feels really silly about the way she acted at the party now, embarrassing you and getting jealous over Theo – she doesn't even like him any more! I'm sure she'll apologize soon . . .'

I gave her a sceptical look.

'She can be a really good friend too, you know . . .'

I thought back to the time when I first met Amber.
'I know she can,' I said. Molly was right, and I **REALLY**
didn't want to have another fight.

'So, what have I missed?' I said, trying to change the
subject to safer territory. 'OMG, I still don't know about
your dates with Josh and Asher!'

She shrugged. 'Not much to say really. We met them
in town, and they ditched us after an hour to go meet
some Year Eight girls.'

'That sucks!'

'Yeh, but whatever – I was never that keen anyway . . .
It was more Amber's idea. How about you? I saw you
talking to Daniel at the party?'

'Well . . .' I began, trying and failing to keep my voice
calm. **'HE ASKED ME ON A DATE!'**

'OMG!!!!!!!!!!!!!!!!'

'I KNOW!!!!!!!!!!!!!'

'I'm **SO** happy for you, Lotts! And guess what!'

'What?'

'THEO ASKED ME ON A DATE TOO!'

'OMG!!!!!!!!!!!!!!!!!'

'I KNOW!!!!!!!!!!!!!'

'Do you know what this means . . . **WE COULD GO ON A DOUBLE DATE!!!!!!!!!'**

And then Mum came in and told me to stop being so noisy as she was trying (unsuccessfully) to get Bella to take a nap. She didn't look cross when she said it though – I think she realized that all the hysterical screaming was a sign that me and Molly were back on good terms.

MONDAY 2 MAY

Good news: it's a bank holiday today, so no school – yay!
Bad news: I'm running out of pages again. I can't believe
I've filled another whole diary up – thank you for coming
along for the ride! It's been fun, right? I'm afraid you'll
have to wait for my next diary to find out about my date
with Daniel . . . EEK, I'm getting so nervous already just
writing it down. I mean . . . what will I wear?! Will we
have enough to talk about?! How do you eat ice cream in
front of a boy you like?! What if I dribble mint choc chip
all down my chin?! What if he tries to kiss me?! **WHAT
IF HE TRIES TO KISS ME WHILE I HAVE MINT
CHOC CHIP ALL DOWN MY CHIN?!?!**

Argh, I'll have to worry about that later because this is the part where I record all my wisdom so that you and me can remember what we've learnt and, let's be honest, probably forget it all again and keep making the same mistakes, but hey ho . . .

Dear Lottie,

A few BIG things have happened in the last few months . . .

You had a lead role in a play, you got your period (while dressed as a crab – not recommended), you got an accidental boyfriend, you had your heart broken, you almost died while getting your ears pierced, you almost lost your BFF but then you realized she'll always be there when you need her ❤, you have a date with a boy who seems to really like you (even though you almost spat burger in his face), and you finally started growing boobs! (TBH they aren't much to write home about, but it's a start.)

Some of those things have been good, some not so good. Some have made you feel happy and some have made you feel pretty sad. One thing is for sure – it's definitely not been dull! Here are a few of the important things that I don't want you (us) to forget.

Friendships change and, although it's hard when you grow apart from someone you were really close to, it's kind of normal when you get to high school.

And who knows? Maybe that friend will end up coming back . . .

But even if they don't . . . new friends can be the absolute bestest!! Hanging out with people you have fun with is the most important thing.

I don't think trying too hard to talk to boys you like EVER works. Maybe you just have to be your own awkward self and if they still like you, then great! And if they don't like you, then they weren't right for you anyway.

It's easy to focus on your own flaws and think they are a huge deal, but do you ever really notice anyone else's Mount Barbara? Nah.

You CAN do big things if you believe in yourself (like get up on stage in front of all those people and make them laugh – wow!).

If you have a pet hamster and you think it's dead, don't bury it immediately – it may just be very lazy.

PS OMG, I can't go without telling you this . . . Mum just shouted up to me, 'Lottie, a card has just arrived for you!'

I ran downstairs and she passed me a plain white envelope with 'LOTTIE' on the front in capitals.

'A handwritten card on a Sunday?' I thought – most peculiar.

I tore it open and grinned . . .

ROSES ARE RED,
MONSTER MUNCH ARE MUNCHIE,
I WONDERED IF YOU'D LIKE TO SHARE MY CRUNCHIE?

Inside it said:

Don't worry, I don't expect half your KitKat Chunky in return. D x

I can't help but think we might be a match made in chocolate-bar heaven!

Until next time . . .

Love Lottie
xxx

DEAR DIARY,

I'm about to start high school without any friends, I have the most boring hair in the world and, worst of all, I'm too flat-chested to wear a bra! Could my life get any worse?

READ THE FIRST DIARY FROM LOTTIE BROOKS FOR MORE EXTREMELY EMBARRASSING ADVENTURES!

HOW WELL DO YOU KNOW LOTTIE BROOKS?

Take this quiz to see how much you know about Lottie's catastrophic life.

1 WHAT IS LOTTIE'S BABY SISTER CALLED?

A   Davina

B   Olivia

C   Bella

2 WHO ENDS UP GETTING THE VALENTINE'S DAY CARD LOTTIE WROTE?

A   Dreamy Daniel

B   Brad the Lad

C   Dan the Man

3 WHAT DOESN'T LOTTIE DO ON SCREEN-FREE SUNDAY?

A   Complete puzzles

B   Play Snakes and Ladders

C   Perfect a TikTok dance

(4) LOTTIE'S FAVOURITE POT NOODLE FLAVOUR IS . . .

A   Chicken and Mushroom

B   Bombay Bad Boy

C   Beef and Tomato

(5) WHO SHOWS UP TO LOTTIE'S SLEEPOVER WITH MOLLY?

A   Leggy Lexi

B   Amber

C   Poppy

(6) WHAT ROLE DOES LOTTIE GET IN *THE LITTLE MERMAID*?

A   King Triton

B   Sebastian

C   Ariel

(7) WHAT DOES LOTTIE NAME HER SPOT?

What a strange girl . . .

A   Mount Barbara

B   Mount Alice

C   Mount Ida

FACT FILES BY LOTTIE BROOKS

NAME:
Lottie

STRENGTHS:

* ★ Choosing
  bubble-tea flavours
* ★ Acting like a singing crustacean
* ★ Scoffing KitKat Chunkys

WEAKNESSES:

* ★ Roller skating
* ★ Talking to cute boys
* ★ Focusing in class

NAME:
Daniel

STRENGTHS:

* Gorgeous

* Really friendly

* Applauded my crustacean
  performance

WEAKNESSES:

* Started going out with Marnie

* Shows up when I'm eating burgers

NAME:
Bella

STRENGTHS:

* Cute

* Smelling like strawberry
  milkshake

WEAKNESSES:

* Poos on people's clothes

* Melodramatic – cries about
  EVERYTHING

KATIE KIRBY is a writer and illustrator who lives by the sea in Hove with her husband, two sons and dog Sasha.

She has a degree in advertising and marketing, and after spending several years working in London media agencies, which basically involved hanging out in fancy restaurants and pretending to know what she was talking about, she had some children and decided to start a blog called 'Hurrah for Gin' about the gross injustice of it all.

Many people said her sense of humour was silly and immature, so she is now having a bash at writing children's fiction.

Katie likes gin, rabbits, over thinking things, the smell of launderettes and Monster Munch. She does not like losing at board games or writing about herself in the third person.